Ending on a Die Note

Ending on a Die Note

A Wedding Bell Mysteries Novel

Nancy Robards Thompson

Ending on a Die Note
Copyright© 2021 Nancy Robards Thompson
Tule Publishing First Printing, October 2021

The Tule Publishing, Inc.

ALL RIGHTS RESERVED

First Publication by Tule Publishing 2021

Cover illustrated by Cortney Langevin Spillane

No part of this book may be used or reproduced in any manner whatsoever without written permission except in the case of brief quotations embodied in critical articles and reviews.

This is a work of fiction. Names, characters, places, and incidents are products of the author's imagination or are used fictitiously. Any resemblance to actual events, locales, organizations, or persons, living or dead, is entirely coincidental.

AI was not used to create any part of this book and no part of this book may be used for generative training.

ISBN: 978-1-954894-77-8

Dedication

This book is dedicated to Isaiah Dufresne. Always remember, you can do anything.

Prologue

~ Maddie ~

Fourth of July

I'M SITTING IN Hemlock's Central Park, watching the fireworks explode all around us in glorious bursts of gold, green, red, blue, and silver. The star-spangled spectacle is set to live patriotic music compliments of the Hemlock Symphony Orchestra. Everyone is rapt and gazing skyward, but despite the humid summer night, a chill ripples through me. I have the strangest feeling that someone is watching me.

I blink a few times to clear my vision, then I scan the crowd.

That's when I see *him*.

My eyes must be playing tricks on me.

But *no*. It is definitely my husband, Frank, the love of my life, who has been missing for nine years. He is standing next to the huge oak tree on the edge of the park, the one where we'd left our mark—Frank loves Maddie—when we were fifteen. The same tree we were standing under the night he got down on one knee and proposed to me when we were eighteen.

Now, after he has been gone for nearly a decade, he stands at that same tree, his hand on the trunk, and he looks like he is waiting for me. He smiles and lifts his hand.

I push to my feet and run toward him, weaving in and out of the patchwork of blankets laid out on the park's lawn, dodging the people lounging on chairs and milling about, standing in my way, and blocking my view. I've lost sight of him. I'm frantic but hopeful. So full of love. Crying and craning my neck, I'm desperate to catch sight of him again— why are so many people standing between us?

If I can just get around them, I know I'll see him running toward me.

Voices call after me, but they sound far away and tinny, as if they are coming from another dimension.

"Maddie? Where are you going?"

"What's wrong, Mom?"

Jack and Jenna…

But I don't stop. I can't stop until I'm in my husband's arms again.

By the time I reach the tree, I'm out of breath and the stitch in my side makes me double over. For a second, I worry that I am having a heart attack.

But then, as I turn in a circle looking for Frank, I realize that the pain I feel is my heart breaking all over again because he isn't there—or anywhere that I can see.

Even though I *know* I saw him. I know it. My body felt

him even before our gazes connected. My broken heart that has missed this man every single day since his plane went down in Afghanistan *knows*.

Frank is gone.

This is his way of finally saying goodbye.

A week later, I am not surprised when the black sedan turns into my driveway.

I've been expecting it. Actually, I thought the navy chaplain would've come sooner. On the other hand, one week waiting for the official word to come down is like the blink of an eye when compared to nine years of worrying and praying over a husband who's been missing in action.

It is official. Frank is dead. That night in the park... I believe he came to give me permission to get on with my life, but even after all this time, the grieving has just begun.

Chapter One

~ Maddie ~

September

OVER THE PAST two months, I've been talking to Frank a lot. He doesn't answer back, of course, because he's dead. The conversations are mostly in my head. Mostly. Except when I get maudlin and start wondering out loud why he left me waiting and wondering and hoping for nine years only to turn up dead in the end.

I'd held out hope all these years because I believed that when I stopped expecting him to walk through the front door of the home we had bought together, that would be the day I quit believing in him.

I guess the joke is on me. Not that Frank would purposely string me along. He was a great guy, and he certainly wouldn't have chosen this ending. But I'm still working through why he could appear to me in the park a week before the officials showed up at my door.

I'm still trying to come to terms with how I could have expected something for so long, yet when the official word finally came, it landed like an unexpected punch to the gut that flattened me.

"Why, Frank?" I ask as I adjust the pearl necklace that I am wearing tonight to the Hemlock Ladies League Harvest Moon Gala. "If you could show up then, why not years earlier?"

He doesn't answer, of course, and I suppose that's a good thing. If my dead husband starts answering my questions, it will signal a whole new level of trouble.

Right before I saw Frank in the park, I had been edging toward moving on with my life. I had even dipped my toe into the pool of possibilities. Okay, so I'd kissed Jackson Bradley. Maybe that was more than testing the waters.

But while the definitive word on my husband's fate should've set me free to move on, to explore the feelings that have been developing between Jack and me, it set me back.

I felt guilty. Like I'd been caught cheating. Even though all I'd done was kiss Jack.

Even though I've waited a long time to take our "friendship" to the next level—as chaste as it is.

I've been so rattled by seeing Frank and the subsequent official word that they'd identified his remains, I pushed Jack away.

When I tell him I need time to figure things out, Jack says he understands. He says he'll give me space, but he'll be here for me when I'm ready.

So how do I repay his kind understanding? I stop returning his calls and texts. I stop going across the street to the Briar Patch Bakery where I used to go every morning to write two pages on the cozy mystery series I've been developing. Where Jack would saunter in every morning just as I was closing my laptop and we would have coffee and conversation.

It started when I asked if I could pick his brain about police procedure for my stories. Gradually, our morning coffee meet-ups morphed into something more personal. Nothing inappropriate, of course. After all, we were in public. But a chemistry brewed between us and developed into an emotional closeness.

It's been two months since we've spoken. I am 100 percent to blame for that because I'm the one who has been avoiding him.

The Hemlock fall celebration kicks off tonight with the Harvest Moon Gala, a black tie soiree. The Family Fall Festival in the park is tomorrow. It's open to the entire town of Hemlock. But tonight's dinner dance is a bit more exclusive because it is a fundraiser for The Hemlock Library.

Jack and I had talked about attending the gala together, but after everything happened, we didn't firm up our plans. I was more than happy to stay home, but my daughter, Jenna, is one of the cochairs of the committee this year, and since her boyfriend, Ian McCoy, will be out of town at a law conference this weekend, she asked me to be her date.

She's worked so hard on the festival, and she has been so

good to me, so patient, I figure the least I can do is come out and support her tonight.

Now, here I am at a community event in my strapless navy blue gown and pearls. Honestly, I can't remember the last time I wore heels in public.

After I walk into the Hemlock Inn in those strappy heels, I'm hit with a ridiculous wave of emotion. I shouldn't be here. I fight with the urge to turn around and leave, but, before I can figure out what I want to do, Jenna sees me across the crowded ballroom and waves. She looks lovely in her pink tulle gown. Like the fairy princess she always wanted to be when she was little. The light color of the gown contrasts with her dark hair and brings out the excited blush of her cheeks. Her approach to grieving the loss of her father has been different from mine. She has stayed so busy that she hasn't had time to mourn.

Then again, she was seventeen when Frank went missing. Not that she gave up on her father, but let's say after nine years with no word from him, she was more realistic that the odds of him returning alive were not in our favor.

Tonight, I hope she needs my help with something—anything—because I need something to do other than standing there feeling out of place.

There is a flurry of excitement in the ballroom—convivial sounds of friends meeting; people floating from station to station bidding on items in the silent auction. On the stage, someone makes last-minute adjustments to instruments that belong to the semi-famous, one-hit wonder band ShakesPierre, who will perform a live acoustic concert tonight. Jenna was able to book them for the entire weekend because the lead singer, Pierre Von Strussen, was a college friend of Jenna's best friend, Tess Harrison, who also happens to be Jenna's cochair for the weekend.

Tess and this Pierre guy may have dated at one point. I don't know the full story, but I do know that Jenna has been able to secure them as the entertainment for both tonight's dinner dance and tomorrow's fall festival. A two-for-the-price-of-one bargain.

"Mom, you look beautiful," Jenna says as she leans in and gives me a quick squeeze. "I'm so glad you're here. Are you having fun?"

"Fun?" I smooth my hands over the skirt of my gown. "I just got here. But everything looks great. Can I help you with something?"

Anything? Please give me a job.

"No, everything is handled. Val is coming tonight. Go find her and have fun."

I affix a smile to my face and hope it doesn't fall, the same way I hope my false eyelashes stay in place and my heel doesn't get caught in the hem of my dress and cause me to make an indecent public spectacle of myself.

Someone calls Jenna's name.

"I've got to run, Mom," she says. "We're at table seven. I'll meet up with you there."

I scan the ballroom for my friend Valorie Anderson, but I don't see her. I called Val yesterday to see if she wanted to arrive together, but she works in real estate and had a late appointment on the schedule. She still isn't here. So I walk around, saying hello to people I know and checking out the silent auction items, looking for things I can't resist.

There is a weekend stay at the Hemlock Inn, the host venue of tonight's soiree. Various and sundry manicures, pedicures, haircuts, and colors. There is a certificate for an oil change, another for a security system, and an offer to cater a dinner party for ten, complements of Tess Harrison, owner of the Briar Patch Bakery, who is just starting her own catering company. Jenna has donated party-planning services from her company, Champaign Weddings and Event Designs. I've contributed a sizable gift certificate to my shop, Blissful Beginnings Bridal Boutique, since I wasn't sure how many bidders would be in the market for a wedding gown and bridal accessories. My boutique also carries eveningwear, so a gift certificate gives the winning bidder choices.

I place bids on several items that don't have any takers as of yet. I figure it will get the party started, or at the very least I will end up with a sixty-minute massage for a steal. Can't beat that.

"Finding anything good?" Finally, Val appears beside me. "You look gorgeous, Mads."

She leans in and kisses my cheek, then she picks up the pen and raises my bid for the massage by five dollars.

"If this weren't for such a good cause, I might be mad at you for trying to outbid me." I take the pen and up the ante another ten dollars.

I also give her the stink-eye.

"Well, it is a fundraiser," Valorie says. "It's for a good cause. Are you here solo tonight?"

Unless you count the ghost of my late husband, who seems to follow me everywhere these days. I nodded. "Why do you think I called you yesterday? I wasn't looking for a third wheel."

Val scoffed. "I'd hoped your plans might've changed and you found a last-minute date to this shindig."

"Jenna is my date. Even if she wasn't who would I come here with besides Jack? And asking him would feel awkward after two months of radio silence on my end."

I make a face at her, but the look on her face—like she has heartburn or something equally unwelcome—suggests she isn't kidding.

"What is it?" I ask.

She glances around the ballroom before she lowers her voice. "Jack is here with a woman I've never seen before. He wouldn't bring a date, would he?"

I tried to ignore the way her words *Jack* and *date* pierce through my ribs. "If he did, good for him."

Despite how I try to fool myself, the thought of him being here tonight with someone else makes me feel… It makes me *feel*. And I'm not ready to *feel*.

I can't stop my gaze from meandering around the ballroom.

"Did you see this?" Valorie asks. "The singer from ShakesPierre is giving away a pair of the bedazzled high-top tennis shoes from the line he's designing."

We silently regard the way the shoes sparkle and glitter under the ballroom lights.

"I wish I'd known about these before tonight, I would've worn them rather than heels," Val says. "My feet are already killing me."

She starts to pick up one of the shoes, but the pair is attached by a plastic tie and tethered to the stand. Even so, there's still enough give that she shoes fall over on their side, and I can make out the loopy signature of Pierre Von Strussen, lead singer turned shoe bedazzler.

"I guess they don't want to take a chance that people will try them on."

I chuckle at the thought of someone hiking up their ball gown to try on the shoe. The image is so Cinderella meets Shoe Carnival.

"Are you going to bid on them?" I ask.

Valorie shrugs and writes down twenty dollars. "Why not? It was good of him to donate a pair for the cause. Even though sparkly sneaks are the last thing I need, it would be embarrassing if no one bid on them.

"Oh, speaking of things I do not need, Derry's Donuts is offering a dozen donuts a week for a year. Did you see that?"

"No, but I haven't made it around to that side of the

room yet."

I suddenly feel riveted to the spot, afraid I may run into Jack and his date if I venture out.

"Did you bid on the donuts?" I ask Valorie.

"Of course I did."

"Good. If I get over there, I'm going to up-bid you on that one, too."

"Well, if you do that, when I win, I won't share," she says as she bids ten dollars for a manicure.

When she puts the pen down, Pierre Von Strussen, the flamboyant designer of the shoes materializes seemingly out of nowhere.

"Ladies," he says. "Allow me to introduce myself. I am Pierre Von Strussen." He places one hand over the middle of his maroon and black velvet smoking jacket and folds his lanky body into a deep bow. After he straightens, he preens for a moment, as if he expects us to fangirl and fawn over him. With his unruly dark hair and intense, thick-lashed eyes, he looks like the love child of Freddie Mercury and Russell Brand. Or maybe Desi Arnaz, because despite his… flair for the unusual, Pierre Von Strussen is a good-looking guy. I can't help but wonder if he had been prone to such theater when Tess knew him in college.

"At least someone in this joint has taste." He straightens the shoes on the display case, regarding his creation as if he is examining a masterpiece. "I was beginning to think no one was going to bid on these lovelies."

He has an affected way of talking that is reminiscent of movies of the 1930s and '40s when actors sounded vaguely British.

"The night's early," Valorie says. "I'm sure people are still making the rounds of the silent auction items. But if I do end up being the only bidder, then lucky me."

I nudge her. "Earlier, someone reminded me that this is a fundraiser." I pick up the pen, prepared to up Val's bid by five dollars. "To that end, I will do my duty."

Pierre suddenly puts his hand over mine. "You're Jenna Bell's mother, aren't you?"

"Guilty as charged," I say.

"You have a lovely daughter, Mrs. Bell."

I can't decide if he sounds like Eddie Haskell or someone's seventy-five-year-old grandpa? "Please call me Maddie."

"Okay, you have a lovely daughter, *Maddie*. And I hear that you have an equally lovely boutique here in town."

"Well, I don't know that my shop is as lovely as my daughter, but I'd like to think the place has charm."

"So I've heard," he says. "Before I leave town with the band, I'd like to talk to you about a potential business opportunity."

"What kind of business opportunity?" I ask, bracing for a multilevel marketing pitch. Because what sort of business opportunity could a rock star shoe designer offer a small-town bridal shop owner?

He raises his head and looks down his aquiline nose at

me. "I happen to have an opening in this region for an exclusive distributorship for Pierre Von Strussen Enterprises. I need someone who has the reputation of being an influencer, if you will."

Valorie snort laughs. "Yes, our Maddie is quite the influencer."

I can't look at her. If I do, I'll start laughing.

"Are we talking shoes or music?" I ask.

"Shoes and general fashion, of course. I doubt you know much about music. Am I correct?"

I raise my eyebrows. "Mr. Von Strussen, I own a bridal boutique. It's hardly the perfect market for your tennis shoes. Even as lovely as they are."

"And this, madame, is hardly an ordinary *tennis shoe*." Again, he adjusts the sneaker on the display cube, moving it this way and that. "I happen to have it on good authority that demand for my brand will soon outweigh the supply. I am potentially offering you a ground-floor opportunity."

"Is that *the* Pierre Von Strussen?" says a woman who is clutching a piece of paper in one hand and a pen in the other. I know most everyone in Hemlock, but I don't recognize her.

Pierre turns around and simpers. "The one and only."

"Oh, it is you!" the woman says. "I am your biggest fan. I can't believe you're here. May I please have your autograph?"

This is the opening I need to make my escape, but as I start to walk away, Valorie leans in and whispers, "Don't turn around. Jack and his date are coming this way."

Of course, that's exactly what I do. I can't stop myself from glancing over my shoulder. Our gazes lock. He smiles and nods, then leans in to hear what the beautiful blonde on his arm is saying.

"Let's go bid on those donuts," I say to Valorie.

Chapter Two

~ Jenna ~

"GOOD EVENING, EVERYONE," I say to the sea of faces in the Hemlock Inn ballroom from my place on the stage. "My name is Jenna Bell. I'm one of this year's cochairs of the Hemlock Harvest Moon Gala and Fall Festival."

The servers are clearing the dinner dishes and bringing out dessert. Behind me, the ShakesPierre band members are taking the stage to perform a special unplugged concert.

"Tess Harrison, my cochair for this evening's event, has been in the kitchen all night ensuring tonight's dinner was delicious. Didn't she do a great job? Tess, are you available to come out here?"

She appears in the doorway that leads to the kitchen, and people break into spontaneous applause. Tess gives a shy wave and bows her head.

As the adulation dies down, someone behind me whistles loudly and unleashes, "Whoo-hoo, Tess! *Yaaas!* That's my girl. Tess Harrison, everyone!"

Lead singer Allan Bossert, better known by his stage

name, Pierre Von Strussen, raises his hand to his mouth and lets loose another loud whistle.

Tess frowns, her face turns red, and she ducks back into the kitchen.

This morning, when I tried to get her to take a break and listen to the band's sound check, she confided that things between her and Allan had ended badly. I wish she would've made that clear before we'd booked the band to play for the gala and festival, she'd assured me she was prepared to take one for the team, since we would be hard pressed to book another band for the price we'd booked ShakesPierre. It was too good of a deal to pass up. She said she'd be busy in the kitchen, and all would be well.

"After what Allan did to me," Tess said this morning, "he probably doesn't want to see me any more than I want to see him. The guy is a jerk and a thief. I'll give you all the details later. In the meantime, please understand if I need to lie low."

I am dying to know what had happened between them.

Now, I'm second-guessing my idea to recognize Tess for the dinner, but she has been working hard to add a catering division to her business, the Briar Patch Bakery. The influencers who are in attendance need to associate her with the delicious food served tonight. It is especially urgent since a competing business has leased the space right next door to the Briar Patch and is opening the first of next month.

Tess deserves the accolades. I do wish Pierre—or Allan or

whatever his name is—hadn't whistled like that.

"The silent auction will close in five minutes," I continue. "While ShakesPierre entertains us, the volunteers will tabulate the bids and notify the winners. If you have your heart set on an auction item, this is your last chance to up the ante."

As several people stand and scatter to various auction items around the room, a guitar strums behind me. The perfect segue to the band.

"Without further ado, I give you ShakesPierre."

Allan—okay, I guess since he is performing, I should call him Pierre—Pierre strums the intro to a song, then stops. "Thanks, Jenna. Everyone, give it up for Jenna Bell and let's have another round for Tess Harrison. The two of them have worked hard putting together this little event."

Out of the corner of my eye, I see Pierre gesture to me, and, feeling the weight of the crowd's gaze on me, I slow, navigating the steps gingerly. I am not graceful on a good day. In this gown and heels… it's a perfect moment for a faceplant. To my great relief, I make it down without incident.

"Tess?" Pierre says. "Paging Tess Harrison. Come out, come out wherever you are."

Oh no. Poor Tess. I don't even have to see her face to know Pierre's summons won't go over well.

"Ladies and gentlemen, I think Tess is ignoring me." Pierre picks out a tune on his guitar as he speaks. "Well, since she's not coming out, I'm going to talk about her until she does. Tess and I met in college. She and I used to sing together. In fact, we had a little band called—"

Suddenly, Tess appears in the doorway, looking drawn and pale.

"There she is!" Pierre claps over his head. The audience starts applauding, too. "Ladies and gentlemen, let's hear it one more time for Tess and Jenna."

She gives a very short salute and turns toward the kitchen.

"Tess, don't go," he says. "Ladies and gentlemen, who here wants Tess to come up and join me in a song? She really is multitalented."

The audience's applause escalates into unified, rhythmic claps. Someone starts chanting, "Tess! Tess! Tess!" Others join in.

"I thought you'd like that," Pierre says. "And, hey, I've got an even better idea. What if we raise even more money for whatever it is you're fundraising for tonight? What do you say we add an item to the silent auction? Jenna, can I do that? Of course I can. I'm your special guest. I can do whatever I want. So how about if the highest bidder gets to choose a song, any song you want, for your very own Tess Harrison and *moi* to sing together at tomorrow night's concert in the park?" Pierre snaps his fingers. "Jenna, be a love and fetch me a piece of paper so people can write down their bids. Come on, everyone. Be generous. This is for a good cause. Maybe someone will choose ShakesPierre's number one song, 'Tsunami.'" He plays the opening strains of the song. "Wouldn't that be fun?"

I start to protest but it's too late. People are standing and looking for where to place their bid.

Frankly, I want to strangle Pierre Von Strussen right now—or, better yet, call him by his real name in front of all these people. *Allan Bossert, you little twit, stop it right now. Does bullying Tess make you feel better about yourself?* Thank goodness the band's manager, Angel Ferguson, approaches me. Angel is my point person, and she is one of the few people who seems to know how to handle Allan/Pierre.

"I don't know if we can do this, Pierre," Angel says, even though he can't hear her. "Tess has to agree."

By this time, Marcy Holden, who is the committee member in charge of the silent auction, has produced a piece of paper and is waving it over her head. "Over here, everyone. Place your bids to hear Tess sing with Pierre Von Strussen right here."

Tess is right about Pierre Von Strussen being a piece of work. It takes a lot of gall to put someone on the spot like that, volunteering her without asking her if she is on board.

"Just say the word and I'll put an end to this," Angel says.

Tall and rail thin, ShakesPierre's manager is pretty, with sleek black hair cut in a chin-length bob with bangs. A style I envy. My hair has too much body—too much of a mind of its own. To that end, my body has too many curves to pull off Angel's simple black silk slip dress. She looks effortlessly stylish. With her crimson lipstick, she is more Fifth Avenue than rock and roll, although the angel tattoo on her left shoulder and her wide, winged eyeliner make it more Fifth Avenue with an edge.

"Let me go talk to Tess," I say.

I turn toward the kitchen, but Tess meets us at the kitchen door, looking murderous and on the verge of tears.

"Who does he think he is?" Her voice is a hoarse whisper that breaks on the last word.

"I'm sorry." I shake my head. "I'm so sorry. You don't have to do this. I can shut it down right now."

From our position in the doorway, we can see the crowd of people who have gathered around Marcy, eager to bid on the surprise item.

"Who knew you'd be the hottest item in the silent auction?" I say, hoping she'll laugh, but she doesn't even crack a smile.

Instead, she shrugs. "Looks like I'm dammed if I do, dammed if I don't, doesn't it?"

Now, I'm even more curious about what happened between Tess and Pierre. I can see that he's a jerk, but what is making him act so passive-aggressively toward Tess after all these years? Obviously, their dispute goes deeper than a run-of-the-mill bad breakup.

Earlier, she'd called him a liar and a thief.

Tess isn't prone to drama or histrionics. She deals with all kinds of people at the bakery every day. Some of those people she likes more than others, but she always manages to serve them with a smile.

This mess certainly isn't Tess's fault. It's one-hundred percent Allan Bossert.

"What do you want me to do?" I ask.

"It's fine," Tess finally says. "Just let it go. Let's see how much money we can raise." Her face is stony.

"Are you sure?" I ask.

"Absolutely. If he wants to play dirty, two can play that game…" Her voice trails off as she realizes Angel is still standing there and some of the staff is nearby.

"George, Sandy, Alexa," Tess says to the three who are the most blatant eavesdroppers, "those glasses need to be dried and packed up. Would you please take care of them?"

The teenagers nod. "Consider it done," George says.

"Thank you." Tess motions with her head for me to follow her to the other side of the kitchen.

"Are you plotting a payback for your old buddy?" Angel shoots Tess a conspiratorial smile.

Tess answers with a noncommittal shrug.

"Tess, for years, I have felt guilty about what happened," Angel says. "I still feel like I owe you an apology."

Tess and Angel knew each other before this festival?

"What happened?" I ask.

Angel looks regretful. "Back in the day when Allan and

Tess played together as the Rambling Roses, I was the A&R exec who discovered them."

Ooh. I know this story, but I didn't realize Angel was the A&R scout. When she brought the band to the record label, her bosses essentially disassembled the Rambling Roses. They brought Allan on board, encouraged him to change his name to Pierre Von Strussen, and formed what they thought was the more marketable ShakesPierre group.

Tess and the other members of the Rambling Roses had been kicked to the curb while Allan Bossert had gotten a record deal by signing on with the company-formed ShakesPierre.

"Tess, you need to know that I fought for you," Angel says. "You were so talented. I thought you and Allan made a great team. Together, you had a sound like none I'd heard and nothing I've heard since. But I was overruled by the bigwigs. I'm sorry it happened that way. Will you please accept my apology?"

"Of course," Tess says. "It was upsetting at the time, but sometimes things happen for a reason. I was not cut out for life on the road. I'm happy."

Angel exhales, and there are tears in her eyes. "I'm so glad to hear that because what happened to you has haunted me every day. It's why I decided to get out of A&R and go into management. I'm not good at breaking people's hearts. I like helping make people's dreams come true. No hard feelings?"

"Absolutely no hard feelings," Tess says. "Well, not toward you anyway. But Allan Bossert… All I'm saying is, I have a score to settle with him, and this performance stunt he is pulling just may be my chance."

Angel's eyes widen. "Should we be worried?"

Before Tess can answer, Marcy Holden approaches. "Ladies, I'm sorry to interrupt, but does anyone have a pair of scissors? I need to cut the plastic security tie that's anchoring the shoes Pierre donated. We have a winner, and she wants to take home her prize tonight."

"I don't have any scissors," Tess says, "but I have a kitchen knife. Would that work?"

"Like a charm," Marcy says.

As Tess turns toward the kitchen, Angel says, "I want to hear more about this fabulous, diabolical plan of yours."

Tess narrows her eyes and smiles. "Let's just say, I'm going to make Allan Bossert regret coming to Hemlock, North Carolina."

Chapter Three

~ Jenna ~

THE RINGING PHONE jolts me out of a sleep so sound that, for a moment, I don't know where I am. I blink a few times, and then I realize the shrill sound that woke me is the ringtone of my phone and not the shrieking vocals of Pierre Von Strussen, who somehow managed to elbow his way into my post-gala dream.

I reach over and glance at the screen. Tess. At 4:17 a.m.

My heart slams against my ribcage.

I fumble to answer, nearly dropping my phone.

"Tess? Is everything okay?"

Silence meets my question, there is a split second when I think maybe Tess has butt dialed me. Then I hear her shaky voice.

"Jenna? I need you to help me. Please come help me."

She is crying.

I bolt upright in my bed. "Tess? What's wrong? What's happened?"

"It's Allan. He's dead."

I swing my feet over the side of the bed and stand, wide awake now.

"What?"

"Allan Bossert is dead."

"Tess, where are you?"

"I'm at the bakery." Her voice sounds far away.

"Where is Allan? Is he there… with you?"

"No. He's in the alleyway between my apartment and the side door of the Briar Patch."

"Are you alone?"

"Yes. At least I think so. I hope so. Jenna, I'm scared. What should I do?"

"Have you called the police?"

"No."

I hate myself, but for a moment, I wonder if she killed Pierre—er, Allan—and that's why she hasn't called the police. Then I mentally kick myself because there is no way Tess is capable of murder. Period. Even after the humiliation he heaped upon her last night.

Then, an even more terrifying thought crowds its way into my head. What if the murderer is still there and Tess is alone and vulnerable?

"Are you inside the bakery?"

She makes a squeak that sounds like an affirmative. She's clearly in shock.

"Tess, listen to me. I need you to make sure the bakery doors are locked. Can you do that?"

"Yes."

"Good. Then, I need you to go lock yourself in the bathroom or somewhere where you know you're the only one in the room. I don't want to scare you, but the killer could still be in the area. I'm going to go upstairs and call the police from my mom's landline. I want you to stay on the phone with me. Okay?"

"Uh-huh."

"Everything is going to be okay," I say, despite the fact that I have never been more uncertain of anything in my life. "Talk to me, Tess. Did you go straight home after you finished up in the kitchen at the gala?"

"Yeah."

I grab a pair of jeans, a sweater, and my bra and bound up the inside steps that connect my bottom floor apartment to my mother's house, which is on the main level. After I moved back from college, she renovated her home to give me a place of my own.

"Did anything seem off or odd to you when you got home?"

"Um. Uh. Allan came to see me."

What?

"He did? Why did he do that?" My hand shakes, as I try to insert the key into the door at the top of the stairs.

I place the phone on my shoulder and use one hand to steady the key and the other to guide it into the lock. It turns. I let myself inside and flip on the lights so not to scare the living daylights out of my mother, who is probably as sound asleep as I was a few minutes ago.

However, despite my intentions to wake my mom up gently, her two corgis, Aggie and Homie, short for Agatha Christie and Sherlock Holmes, spring into watchdog mode and start barking.

I press my finger to my lips. "*Shhhhhh*!" As if that will make them stop.

"He said he wanted to talk to me." Tess's small voice continues, despite the cacophony of barks and my hissed whispers.

"Did you let him in?" I ask.

"No."

Okay, that's good.

"What time did Allan come to your door?"

"I had just drifted off to sleep," Tess said. "I heard someone knock and I thought that maybe you were at the door. Or maybe there was some kind of emergency."

"What time was that, Tess?"

"It was around 3:00 a.m."

"Jenna, what in the world is going on?" My mother stands in front of me, squinting and looking groggy and worried. The corgis are alternately jumping up on my legs and licking my bare feet.

I shake my head and hold up a finger.

"Tess, hold on a second. My mom is here. Let me fill her in on what's happened. I'm right here if you need me." Even though I'm a good ten minutes away from downtown where Tess's bakery is located.

I give my mom the quick recap.

"You stay on the phone with her," she says. "Tell her not to worry. I'll call Jack at home and send him over there."

~ Maddie ~

My heart thumps as I hit the speed dial button with Jack's number.

Despite everything that transpired over the past two months, I haven't deleted it. Keeping it isn't really a conscious decision. Or maybe it is. It doesn't matter now. I'm glad I didn't—well, I'm glad for the convenience.

But poor Tess.

Poor Allan.

"Maddie, what is it?" The gentle urgency in Jack's voice startles me.

Or maybe it's his lack of irritation, after everything—me asking for my space and then the way I basically... what was that word Jenna used? *Ghosted* him. Until now. At nearly 4:30 on a Saturday morning. After not even saying hello last night.

Even as I explain to him what happened, in the back of my mind, I wonder if the pretty blonde who had been with him at the gala is in his bed as we speak. But he immediately springs into cop mode, asking the who, what, when, where questions and acting as if it hasn't been nearly two months since we've spoken.

Then again, this isn't about me. This is about Tess and that poor, hapless singer.

Is he really dead? I shiver at the thought.

He was so alive just hours ago.

"Are you and Jenna at home?" Jack asks. "Well, obviously you are since you called from your landline. But Jenna? Is she okay?"

"She's here with me, Jack. Tess called her from the bakery."

Jack is such a good guy. On any other occasion, his concern for my daughter would touch me deeply, but I am sick with worry over Tess.

"Okay, I need to go so I can call for backup and get over there."

"Thank you, Jack. Let us know how we can help. Tess is traumatized."

"For now, the best thing you can do is to stay put," Jack says. "At least until we figure out what we're dealing with. There's a killer on the loose, Maddie. I want you and Jenna to stay safe."

"You be safe, too," I say.

As I hang up the phone, I try to ignore the tug at my heart. It's a foreign feeling that's breaking through the cloaking fog of horror, but it is swiftly pushed aside by the terrifying reality that Pierre Von Strussen—er, Allan Bossert—who had been so full of life last night is dead, and another murder has happened in Hemlock.

The third one in two years.

What is happening to our tiny, close-knit community?

"Jack is on his way." Jenna has put Tess on speaker phone. "How are you doing, honey?" I ask her.

"I'm scared, Maddie." Her voice shakes.

"I know, Tess. I wish we could be there with you, but Jack will be there any minute. Do you have any idea who would do this?"

"No," she squeaks. "But what I'm the most afraid of is that Jack's going to think I did it because Allan's blood is on my sweater."

"What?" Jenna and I say simultaneously.

"What are you talking about? How did his blood get on you?" we both ask, talking over each other.

"When I saw Allan lying there, I bent down to see if I could help him. It's still dark outside, and he was on his stomach. I didn't see the blood until after I turned him over."

"How did he die?" I ask.

"I don't know. There was just so much blood. I'm covered in his blood. It's on my sweater, on my hands, under my nails…"

Tess starts crying. Jenna and I look at each other.

Tess and Jenna have been friends since preschool. She is

like a daughter to me. But, wow, the circumstances don't look good. Last night at the gala, she made no pretense about the fact that she was angry at Allan. I can't blame her after he put her on the spot like that.

In the background, we hear sirens.

"I think Jack's here," Tess says. "I'm still locked in the bathroom. I have to go let him into the bakery."

"Be careful," Jenna says. "Open the bathroom door slowly and be as quiet as you can. In case the killer is still there. Did you hear anything that sounded suspicious while you were waiting?"

"No," Tess says. "Nothing."

We hear the sound of someone pounding on the door.

"Is that Jack?" I ask.

"Yes. He's knocking, and another squad car just pulled up. I'm letting them in."

A moment later, Tess says, "Okay, the police are here. I need to go."

After the call ends, neither of us says a word. Aggie is leaning against my leg, and Homie looks up at me and unleashes a mournful corgi yodel. The dogs are so sensitive, they know when something is wrong. The empathy is one of the things I love about the breed.

"Do you know what was behind the awkwardness last night between Tess and Allan?"

Jenna gives a one-shoulder shrug. "I don't know the details of what happened between them. Tess said she would tell me later, but things got so crazy, we haven't had a chance to talk about it. I wish she'd confided in me before I hired ShakesPierre to perform this weekend. I thought it would be a good thing, but obviously not." Jenna pales and shakes her head. "This looks bad for Tess, Mom. She admitted she had a score to settle with Allan Bossert. And after he pulled that stunt last night, she said she was going to make him regret coming to Hemlock, North Carolina. Her words, not mine."

She closes her eyes and swallows hard.

"And I'm not the only one who heard her say it."

Chapter Four

~ Jenna ~

Mom doesn't want me to go to the crime scene, but Tess has always been there for me. I need to be there for her. We share an almost sisterly connection, and she needs me now if only for moral support.

When my mom sees that there is nothing she could do to dissuade me from going, she decides that since she's up and awake, she may as well go into her shop, which is right across Main Street from Tess's bakery.

We arrive just as the EMTs close the ambulance's doors, but not before I catch a glimpse of two medics hunched over a gurney. Then they drive away without their sirens.

My mom shivers and hugs herself. The frosty fall air isn't the sole cause of her chills.

"I'm going to let myself in the front door of the shop." She gestures absently to her bridal boutique, but her gaze is fixed on Jack. "I would just be in the way, but Tess needs you. Call me if either of you need anything."

She slips away before Jack even realizes she is here.

It's still dark outside, which makes the flashing red and blue lights of the emergency vehicles look even more ominous. The door to the Briar Patch has been cordoned off with yellow crime-scene tape that stretches across the alleyway between Tess's bakery and the storefront next door. The proprietors rented the space last week, and according to the local Gossip Brigade, a competing French bakery will open its doors at the first of the month.

Officers are combing the area for clues. Tess is sitting sideways in the back of a patrol car with her feet on the sidewalk. Chief Jack Bradley is talking to her and jotting down notes in a small notebook. Tess looks dazed as she stares off into the middle distance. Like she isn't present. I want to hug her despite the way her apricot-colored sweater is stained reddish-black with what I presume is Allan Bossert's blood.

Jack looks up and catches my gaze. He smiles and waves me over. "We're finished here. I think she could use a friend right now."

I have a million questions, but now isn't the time to ask. Thank goodness, despite the blood stains on Tess's sweater, Jack is releasing her. Not hauling her down to the station.

Still, I can't help but ask him, "Do you have any idea who did this?"

He sighs and glances at Tess before taking a few steps away from the patrol car. "It's early yet, and I really shouldn't discuss the case, Jenna."

"*But?*" I finish for him.

Even at this hour, a crowd of bystanders has gathered on the sidewalk. I recognize Janey Powers standing in front of her shoe store, two doors down from the Briar Patch, dressed in a robe and slippers. Similar to Tess, she lives in the apartment above her store. The flashing lights and hubbub have, no doubt, awakened her. She is standing next to a man I don't recognize, but he's fully dressed. It registers that I saw them together at the gala last night.

I don't really care about Janey's love life—as far as I am concerned, she can have a different man over every night and I won't judge—but if the circumstances were reversed and Janey had seen a man leaving Tess's apartment in the wee hours of the morning, she would've delighted in sharing that juicy little nugget with the Gossip Brigade, Hemlock's gossipmongers. As it is, she will, no doubt, be reporting on everything she's seen tonight from her front-row station on the sidewalk.

But Janey doesn't have the exclusive on this one.

My gaze is drawn to a car stopped at the traffic light at Main Street and Catalpa Avenue. The Briar Patch is located at that the northeast corner of that intersection. I don't recognize the car, which is idling despite having the green light. There is no traffic at this hour, so he isn't holding up anyone.

It takes a moment, but I finally realize the guy looking out the driver's side window is one of the Collins brothers, the identical twins who are opening Four Seasons Patisserie. Tess and I refer to them as the Co Bros. because if it isn't bad enough that they are opening a competing business right next door to her bakery, they seemed quite snobbish and uninterested in being neighborly when Tess introduced herself.

I squint at him, trying to discern which Co Bro is lurking in the car. Both brothers were at the gala. They donated a gift certificate for their patisserie.

When the Collins brother in the car catches me watching him, he speeds off, making a left turn and driving away.

"Did you see that?" I ask Jack.

"See what?" he says.

"That car that was idling at the intersection. I think it was one of the Collins brothers." I nod at the dark storefront that is further obscured by paper with multiple Eiffel Towers and illustrations of café tables boasting baguettes, croissants, and steaming cups of coffee all arranged around a promise that the patisserie will be opening October first.

Jack follows my gaze and then looks toward the empty intersection.

He shrugs. "Probably just curious about what's going on."

"And why is he here at 5:00 a.m. on a Saturday morning after being out late at the gala last night?" I ask.

"I have no idea, Jenna," he says. "Can you enlighten me?"

Several crazy theories run through my brain. Maybe killing Allan is part of a diabolical plan to disrupt Tess's business, for instance, but as I silently test each theory, each one sounds more ridiculous than the last.

"I don't know," I say. "I'm just making note of everyone who is here at the crime scene this morning."

"Like you?" Jack chuckles. He's just yanking my chain. But he does jot something in his notebook.

"I'm going to trust you to look after Tess until we can get more information," Jack says.

An officer is settling a blanket around her shoulders. She still hasn't given any indication that she even knows I'm here. Why would I need to look after her? If Jack is concerned for her safety, he would assign police protection.

"Um. Okay. Of course, I'll do that."

As I look at Tess's dazed face and her blood-covered sweater, I have a sinking feeling where he is going with this. Still, I'm not about to open that line of conversation. Instead, I hedge.

"Are you afraid that the killer might think Tess is a witness? If that's the case, she can stay with my mom and me. She'll be safe with us."

Jack regards me stoically.

Finally, he says, "You're Tess's best friend. Please make sure she doesn't do anything stupid, like try to leave town."

"Jack, why would she leave town? But if she wanted to, why not? She's not a suspect, is she?"

"Right now, we want to talk to everyone who came into contact with Allan Bossert. I'm considering everyone a potential suspect until they're cleared."

Okay, I guess that includes me. I sigh. I've been down that road before.

To change the subject, I say, "Have you talked to any of these people who are standing around?" I wave my hand. "They might have seen something."

"We will get to them."

Jack's radio squawks and he walks away to answer it, leaving me to look after Tess, who is now sitting alone with the itchy-looking drab olive blanket covering her blood-stained sweater. I walk over and kneel in front of her.

"Tess, are you okay?"

She shakes her head, and her eyes well with tears. "Can we go somewhere?" she asks. "I think the police are in my apartment, but I don't know what they're looking for. Do they think I did this? I didn't do this, Jenna."

"*Shhhhh,*" I say, and I swipe at the tears rolling down her cheeks. "I know you didn't. And I believe Jack knows you didn't do it. He's just following proper police procedure. Let's go over to the bridal shop. My mom is there. We can get you a change of clothes and—"

"Actually, we need to take that sweater in as evidence," Jack says.

I haven't realized he's standing behind me again. For some reason, it feels like he is lurking. Has he been eavesdropping?

I frown at him. "Okay, well, she's certainly not going to whip off her sweater out here on the sidewalk in front of everyone, and her apartment is crawling with cops. What do you suggest, Jack?"

He regards me again with that same expressionless look he'd worn moments ago.

"I heard you say you could get her a change of clothes from your mom's shop. I'll go over there with you and bag the sweater."

"So, you were eavesdropping," I say.

He shakes his head. "No, I just came over to tell you that I need to take Tess's sweater, before you left with her."

"Yeah, you already mentioned that," I say as I take out my phone to text my mom a warning that Jack is coming with us.

Chapter Five

~ Maddie ~

My heartbeat kicks up when I see Jack leaning on the wrap stand in the middle of my shop, looking like he belongs here. Well, as much as a tall cop with honey-brown hair, mahogany eyes, and a sturdy, broad-shouldered body belongs in a bridal boutique.

A shy, uncertain smile curves up the corners of his mouth.

That look says everything, and it makes me feel simultaneously happy to see him and sad to know things are still weird between us.

"Hi, Jack," I say.

"Hi, Maddie," he says. "Sorry to bother you. I need to take in Tess's sweater. For evidence. Jenna said you would have something she could wear."

"You're not bothering me."

Jenna whisks Tess into a fitting room. I haven't gotten a look at Tess's sweater because it's covered by the blanket draped over her shoulders.

Poor Tess.

I remember what Jenna went through a year and a half ago when her ex-boyfriend, Riley Buxston, was killed. The unfortunate incident was Hemlock's first murder since its incorporation as a town more than 130 years ago. Losing Riley turned the town upside down and was especially hard on us because Jenna was considered a prime suspect—until she and I worked together to prove her innocence.

Maybe it's the cozy mystery author in me, but my gut tells me we might need to do the same for Tess. She isn't capable of murder. I know it the same way I knew my daughter was innocent. I want to tell this to Jack, who is paging through his notebook, but I can't find the words.

A moment later, Jenna shepherds Tess back to the wrap stand where Jack and I wait in awkward silence. Tess is wearing a T-shirt with BRIDE TO BE emblazoned in hot pink sequins—a pair of Pierre's bedazzled shoes would go perfectly with the shirt.

Before the Fourth of July, Jack and I might've joked about the spangly ensemble, but this morning, I keep the observation to myself.

Jenna hands Jack what looks like a giant zippered plastic bag. "Thank you," he says. "Tess, I'll be in touch. Maddie, Jenna, take care."

He turns to go.

Maybe it's a reflex, or maybe after seeing him with the blonde at the gala and the two of us acting as if we've been nothing to each other, but I go after him.

"Jack, may I make you a cup of coffee?" I offer. "It's cold out there."

He stops at the door and turns. "That's nice of you, Maddie, but I have a thermos in my car. I need to get back to work."

He gives me that same, sad smile from before, and it pierces my heart like a white-hot poker. There is nothing like a murder to make you realize how short life is. You'd think getting confirmation that my husband is dead would have the same effect, but somehow it hit me the opposite way. I've pushed Jack away. He's only giving me what I want—exactly what I asked for.

"Can we talk sometime?" I hear the words coming out of my mouth before they register in my brain.

He closes his eyes for a moment and scrunches them, no doubt searching for a way to let me down easily—because unlike yours truly, Jack isn't the type to do or say anything that mean even though it would serve me right.

"I just thought…" I start, not entirely sure what I am trying to say. "I just miss talking to you."

Ugh. That is lame. It is true; I do miss him. Shortly after he arrived in Hemlock to take over the job as the chief of police, Jack and I started meeting for coffee right across the street at Tess's bakery. It started innocently enough; he agreed to serve as my expert source, allowing me to bounce all the policing questions that came up as I wrote my cozy mysteries—my side hustle when I'm not selling bridal and formal wear. I've written several books, but I haven't yet found a publisher. That's fine. My favorite joke is that once I do get published, I'll have so many books, I'll be the longest in-the-making overnight sensation the mystery world has ever seen.

"Sure," he says. "I'd like that. Give me a call when you're ready. You should lock the door behind me. There's a killer on the loose."

He lets himself out, leaving the ball squarely in my court.

As I turn the bolt on the glass door, I watch him walk across the street. He is open to talking. I should be relieved.

Am I relieved?

I don't know what I am feeling. There's still the guilt and the grief over Frank. There is the horror over what had happened to Tess and that singer.

At the very least, Jack and I can be friends and I can have my police source back.

My stomach knots at the thought. Jack and I can't go back to being just friends.

I haven't even realized until now that writing—or the researching that facilitates the writing—has been my excuse to see Jack every morning. At first, we'd forged a solid friendship out of those early morning coffee meetings. Then, two months ago, the line between friendship and… more had blurred and… well, we'd gone there. Then I thought I saw—no, I *know* I saw Frank in the park, even if it was just some sort of specter.

It's ridiculous, because I know that my moving into a romantic relationship with Jack isn't the cause of Frank's death. He's been dead a long time. But the timing of what happened in the park and getting confirmation… It's opened everything up. I have to grieve all over again.

Why do I have to keep breaking my own heart, grieving Frank anew, treating Jack like a stranger?

What good is it doing?

I can't answer that question yet. What I do know is my heart isn't ready to move on, but I don't want to lose Jack.

"Mom, I'm making some coffee," Jenna calls from the office, which is in the back of the shop. "Would you and Jack like some?"

"Jack had to go back to work," I say as I turn off the lights in the front of the store and make my way back to join them. We won't open until ten o'clock. There is no sense in leaving the lights on.

When I enter the office, Tess looks like a zombie sitting hunched over in a chair next to Jenna's desk. My daughter operates her event-planning business out of my shop, so she and I share an office.

"How are you doing, honey?" I ask.

Tess blinks as if she's waking up from a long sleep. She shivers and crosses her arms over her middle.

Her eyes fill with tears. "Allan is dead," she says. "I can't believe he's dead."

Jenna arrives with three steaming mugs on a tray, which

she sets on her desk. She hands the first cup of coffee to Tess.

"It's not as good as what you brew at the bakery," Jenna says, "but it will warm you up."

"I don't know if I'll ever feel warm again," Tess says as my daughter hands a cup to me and takes one for herself. "It's not the insult of Jack considering me a suspect, it's that this is so damn typical of Allan to make his exit and leave me holding the bag. I mean, I know he didn't plan to die tonight, but you have to admit the irony is overwhelming."

As she bends her head and sips her coffee, her words twig something.

"You're right," I say. "The irony is pretty overwhelming. Jenna said that you and Allan had a troubled past. Is that right?"

Tess nods.

"Who else knows about your history?"

Tess blinks. "I don't know. The ShakesPierre band is completely different than when we played together in college. ShakesPierre was put together by the record company."

She scoffs, gives a quick shake of her head, and sips her coffee again.

"What?" I ask.

Tess waves me away. "It's not important."

"Everything is important right now, Tess. Because if you didn't kill Allan, I think someone is trying to set it up to look like you did. We need to work together to get to the bottom of this before you're framed for murder."

Chapter Six

~ Jenna ~

TESS LOOKS BETTER after I get her to eat some breakfast. I ordered takeout from the Jay Bird diner and brought it back to the office. I am heartened by her appetite. After bacon, egg, and cheese on a croissant and two cups of strong coffee, she seems more like herself, despite the ridiculous, sparkly bride-to-be T-shirt.

"I know you haven't had a chance to process things, but we need to talk about who might want Allan dead."

Tess runs a hand over her eyes, then shrugs.

My mom pushes her desk chair closer to Tess and sits. She put her hand on Tess's shoulder. "Honey, I know this is difficult, but if we're going to help you, we need you to tell us why you and Allan ended on such bad terms. The investigators are bound to dig it up. What happened?"

Tess makes a face and closes her eyes for a moment—it looks as if she's summoning every ounce of strength she possesses. When she opens her eyes, she gives a resolute nod.

"Allan and I met in college," she says. "We had a chorus

class together, we became good friends, and that eventually developed into something more. I shared with him some of the music I'd written, and he was super complimentary. It was his idea to form the Rambling Roses and perform my songs. He said they deserved to be heard. Then he started writing some of his own. Really, he wasn't very good at it, but his personality was what got us bookings all over Asheville. We sort of became local celebrities. You remember, Jenna."

I nod. "I do. Every time I'd come to see you, you and the band had a gig to play. I remember that Allan was never around much."

"Yeah, for the sake of the band's popularity, he thought it was best for us to keep the fact that we were dating on the down low."

"To be honest, I always thought it was odd that you two acted so casual in public. Sometimes I forgot you were a couple. Not that you had to make out to prove a point, but I always got the feeling that something wasn't right. And for the record, I'm not judging. We've all fallen for at least one player who took us for a ride. Mine was Riley Buxston. So don't feel bad."

Tess's smile looks full of regret.

I know my friend well enough to know that she's holding back.

"And what are you not telling me?"

"You already know all about the A&R thing," Tess says.

"What's A&R?" my mom asks.

"A&R is a scout from a record company who searches for talent. They go to bars and festivals and look for diamonds in the rough. I don't know if it's still the same; I've been out of the music scene for years, but that's how it was back when I was gigging with Allan."

She tells my mother how Angel discovered the band. She laughs, and it sounds a little bitter.

"Were you upset that you were pushed out?" Mom asks. "I mean, Allan went on to find a modicum of fame with ShakesPierre. Were you mad at him for going on without him?"

"I wasn't mad at Allan about *that*." Tess takes the Styrofoam to-go container her breakfast came into the trash.

Mom and I glance at each other. I'd always assumed that Tess and Allan broke up after he quit the Rambling Roses and went to ShakesPierre, and she'd just moved on.

"What were you mad about?" Mom asks.

Tess sits down with a resigned huff but doesn't answer.

"Were you upset because he ditched you for fame and fortune?" she presses.

Tess shifts in her seat. "I don't know if you'd call being a one-hit wonder fame and fortune. But it would've been nice to have had my cut."

"Your cut?" I ask. "Do you mean your chance?"

"No, I mean my *cut*. I wrote the song 'Tsunami,' ShakesPierre's one hit that put them on the map."

"He stole your song?" I ask.

"That's my version of the story. He claimed he wrote it. I know that's a lie. I wrote the song, but I have no proof. What was I going to do, take him and the record company to court? I can see it now. Me against a team of corporate lawyers."

"Tess, I'm sorry," I say. "How come you never told me?"

"Because it's embarrassing. And think about it. It sounds spiteful and bitter. The professionals deemed dorky Tess Harrison not cool enough for their label. They rejected me, so I sue them for vengeance. That was the kind of attention I didn't want. You know I have no problem standing up for myself, but I didn't want to go bankrupt pursuing an impossible lawsuit. I was fine with moving on with my life, turning off the radio or television when 'Tsunami' came on or when I saw Allan Bossert's lying, thieving face."

"He stole from you," Mom says. "I'm sorry about that. It had to hurt."

Tess lifts one shoulder and lets it fall. "Let's address the elephant in the room. Yes, I was mad and hurt. I felt betrayed. As far as I was concerned, if I never saw that creep again, all the better. For the sake of full disclosure, I didn't realize how much I despised him until he and his freak show landed in Hemlock. I thought I was over it, that he could perform, the ladies league could raise money for the library, and I could avoid him. Obviously, I was wrong. Allan was dead set on rubbing my nose in the fact he was a rock star and I was the hired help in the kitchen.

"Do you see the rub? I was damned no matter what I did. He wanted to humiliate me, and that's exactly what he would've done if I'd agreed to sing with him. And if I refused to get on stage with him, I would've been the bad guy who cost the library. But let me be clear: I don't care how mad I was, I would never murder him over it."

We all sit in silence as the enormity of Tess's bombshell settles around us.

"This sounds bad, doesn't it?" Tess says.

"Um, well…" Mom says. "If you look at it a certain way, it could appear rather damning. But let's back up. You went home right after the gala, right?"

Tess nods.

"What time did you get home?" I ask.

"It was 1:30. I know that because I set the alarm to get up at 4:00 to go down to the bakery to get things ready for the Saturday morning rush."

Mom writes the time on the whiteboard.

"What time did Allan come to your door?" Mom asks.

"It was 3:03 a.m.," she says.

"And how do you know this?" I ask.

"Because the sound of him pounding on my door jolted me awake, and I looked at the clock. I was afraid there might be an emergency if someone was knocking so insistently at that hour."

After recording the info on the board, Mom asks, "What

did he want, Tess? What did you talk about?"

The corner of Tess's mouth lifts in disgust. "He was drunk. I mean slurring, stumbling drunk. It was sickening. He wanted to come in to talk about old times. There was no way I was going to let him in."

"But you talked for ten minutes?" I say. "Why not just close the door in his face?"

"I did, but he kept knocking. I was afraid he was going to wake up the neighbors. Now I wish he would've. Maybe he'd still be alive."

"I know." Mom and I glance at each other, and I can tell she's thinking the same thing I'm thinking. This doesn't look good for Tess.

Tess must've caught the exchange. "I did not murder Allan Bossert. He has already taken enough from me. The last thing I'd do would be give up my freedom for that kind of savage revenge."

"We know you didn't," I say. "But it's good that you're talking through all this because we need to know exactly what we're dealing with. That's the only way we can get ahead of this."

"Now we need to figure out who would be so mad at Allan that they would resort to murder," Mom says. She erases the whiteboard in our office and picks up a dry erase marker.

"Who else would want Allan dead?" she asks.

We sit in silence.

"Honestly, I have no idea. Like I told you, the guy hasn't been in my life since he walked away from the Rambling Roses."

"Well, that might be a good place to start," I say. "Can you give us the names of your old band members? Allan gave them the shaft, too. Do you know if any of them would feel particularly vengeful?"

Tess blows out a breath. I can see the wheels turning in her head. "Gosh, we all went our separate ways. I haven't been in touch with any of them since college graduation. Well, except for social media. Although I only have time to concentrate on socials for the bakery. I don't have personal pages. But you know what? I think two of the former band members follow the Briar Patch. Let me check."

She pulls her phone out of the back pocket of her jeans and starts scrolling.

"Yes, here we go. Paul Wentworth… he was the bass player, and… Graham Hollings played guitar. I was the drummer. So, not counting Allan, that was the band."

Mom and I gather around Tess as she clicks on Paul Wentworth's social media page.

"It says Paul lives in Encino, California. He's a recording engineer at Berkside Records. So, he's still in the business."

I jot down Paul's name, then do a web search for his employer's phone number. "Got it," I say, and dial the number. It is Saturday, but it's worth a try.

A guy answers.

"Hey there, this is Lucy Strong," I say. "I was supposed to meet with Paul Wentworth yesterday. Or at least I think I was. Honestly, I can't remember if it was supposed to be yesterday or next Friday. Do you have any idea if he was waiting for me—probably cursing the ground I walked on thinking I stood him up?"

I giggle, trying to sound every bit the airhead I'm trying to portray.

"Paul has been in sessions all week," says the guy. "I doubt that your meeting was yesterday. If you'll hang on, I'll ask him if it's next week. What's your name again?"

"Oh, no, please don't bother him. If he was busy in the studio yesterday, then that probably means we're on for next week. *Phew*! I'm so relieved. And I'm so embarrassed. Do me a favor, please forget I called. I don't want him to think I'm a flake."

I hang up. "Well, Paul Wentworth was in session all the way across the country yesterday. So, I'd venture to guess he wasn't in Hemlock this morning. What was the other guy's name? The guitar player."

"Graham Hollings," Tess says.

My mom crosses through Paul Wentworth's name on the whiteboard and writes Graham Hollings underneath.

"His page isn't quite as forthcoming as Paul's. He doesn't list any personal information. Let me do an internet search."

We wait while Tess looks.

She sighs. "I'm not really coming up with anything. And

Graham Hollings isn't really a common name. Wait—here's something. It's one of those paid information sites where you can search for people's info. What I can see is that he lives in Durham, North Carolina. That's what... about four hours away?"

"It is. Does it say anything else?" Mom asks.

"Just his age. He's twenty-eight. But that's all. If we pay, they'll tell us his address, sex offender status, and whether he has a police record or any other outstanding warrants."

My mom writes *Durham, North Carolina*, next to Graham's name. She follows that with *four hours away*, which she underlines.

"Do you remember how Graham felt about being left behind by Pierre?" I ask. "Was he mad at him?"

"Well, he wasn't happy. None of us were. We all felt a little used. Like Allan had tossed us away when we couldn't help him anymore. But, wait. I don't feel good about this. Just because Graham lives within driving distance doesn't mean he murdered Pierre," Tess says. "I mean I didn't do it, but I don't feel good about turning the cops after someone else who might be innocent."

"We're not accusing Graham of anything," I say. "We're just trying to rule him out or establish a means and motive. Please don't get upset."

"This whole thing is upsetting," Tess says. "I wonder if he even knows that Allan is dead?"

"How do you feel about messaging him through his social media page?" Mom asks.

"That's a heck of a message to leave someone," Tess says. "'Hey, Graham, it's been a long time. Guess what? Allan is dead.' I don't see how that's going to prove anything."

"What if you asked him to call you?" I suggest. "I mean, another way to look at it is, it might be better to hear the news from someone he knows rather than hearing it in the news. I'm assuming the press will catch wind of the story and post it by the end of the day."

Tess doesn't look happy, but she nods. "You're probably right."

"That way, you can hear his voice and assess how he sounds," Mom says.

Tess's thumbs fly over her phone keyboard. "Okay. Done. I said, hi, long time no talk. Then I said I had some news and asked him to call me."

"Good." My mom and I say the word simultaneously. Then the three of us sit in expectant silence, watching Tess's phone as if it will ring instantly.

After a few moments, Tess closes out of her cell and turns it over on her leg. "He may not even get the message." There's an edge to her voice, and she crosses one leg over the other, bouncing it up and down. "Or it might be days before he checks his social media since it doesn't seem like he's very active. I mean, who even has time for that?"

She stands suddenly. "All I want to do right now is sleep. Maybe then I'll be in a better headspace for the festival tonight."

"You've been through a lot," Mom says. "Sleep is probably the best thing for you right now. We can get back to this later."

"And I need to get in touch with Mayor Dobbins and see what he wants to do about the festival," I say. "Not only are we short a band for tonight's concert, but we can't lose sight of the fact that there's been another murder in Hemlock. I'm not quite sure of the best way to proceed. Does the show go on, or do we cancel out of respect to Allan Bossert?"

"That's a good question," Tess says. "Will you let me know so I can update the staff I hired for tonight?"

"Yes."

Tess hesitates and looks a little sheepish. "I have one more favor to ask."

"Sure," I say. "Anything."

"Can I crash at your place? With all that's happened, I'm not comfortable at my apartment."

"Absolutely," I say. "I'll drive you."

As we walk out of the office into the shop, Jack Bradley knocks on the glass front door.

My mom lets him in.

"What's going on, Jack?" she asks.

His frown deepens, and he looks ashen. "I'm sorry to do this, but Tess, I need you to come to the station with me. We believe we have found the weapon used in Allan Bossert's murder. It's a chef's knife. We found it in the bushes outside of your apartment."

Chapter Seven

~ *Maddie* ~

A COUPLE OF hours after Tess leaves with Jack, and Jenna goes to city hall to sort out tonight's festival, my phone rings. "Mom, you're not going to believe this, but not only is the festival happening, ShakesPierre is insisting on playing tonight."

"Are you serious?"

"Serious as murder," Jenna says. "Apparently, the Hemlock police informed the band that they needed to stay put until all statements are completed and some tests come back from the lab. Since they can't leave, they figured they might as well play."

"Right, it's not surprising that Jack asked them to stay." I get up from my desk to make another cup of coffee.

If I were smart, I'd follow Tess's lead and go home for a nap before tonight's festival, but I'm too rattled. I might as well keep busy. Before Jenna called, I'd been in the middle of placing an inventory order that needed to be submitted by the end of the day. Now, the news of the band's eagerness for the show to go on has started an itch I need to scratch.

"I do find it odd that they're so keen to perform," I say. "It hasn't even been twenty-four hours since Allan died."

"You and I are on exactly the same page," Jenna says. "Get this—when I spoke to Titania Blanca, the woman who sings with the band, she said the band had collectively decided that playing the concert would be the best way to honor Allan. But then when I talked to the bass player, Nick Park, he said they really weren't up to going on, but Titania was eager to have the spotlight to herself."

"That's interesting. The lead singer dies, giving another singer a chance to step into the limelight. Ambition isn't a crime, but... *Hmm.* How did she seem when you talked to her?"

"I spoke with her on the phone," Jenna says.

"What if you and I pay Ms. Blanca a visit?" I ask.

"You took the words right out of my mouth," she says.

Jenna meets me at the bridal shop and we drive to the house where the band is staying while they are in town for the Harvest Moon Festival.

On the way, Jenna gets a call from Tess saying that she's heard back from Graham Hollings. He's on tour with a Django Reinhardt tribute band playing in Europe, which probably eliminates him as a suspect.

I make a note to mention it to Jack the next time I see him so that he can follow up and confirm Hollings's alibi.

ShakesPierre had asked the fall festival committee to rent

them a house rather than putting them up in a hotel. Preferably, one without neighbors so they could jam without disturbing anyone. Bruce Flowers, the grandson of Lyle and Betsy Flowers, had inherited his grandparents' house after they passed. It's located off of Old Whickham Road about five miles out of town, and after some ado with Hemlock's zoning committee, he prevailed and turned it into a short-term rental.

It is rather perfect for situations like this, I think as I steer the car up the gravel drive that leads to the house. The old clapboard farmhouse is set back off the highway and situated in the midst of several acres of land, which means the nearest neighbor is at least a mile away. The band could jam to its heart's content without disturbing a soul. It would also be perfect for parties.

"You should talk to Bruce," I say. "This place would make a great venue for weddings."

Jenna grimaces. "After what happened to Allan, doesn't it feel a little tainted now?"

"He didn't die here," I say, surprised by my daughter's squeamishness. She's usually one to forge ahead.

"I know he didn't, but he could've," Jenna says. "Do you think the killer planned that all along? Maybe that's why they wanted such an isolated place. Maybe he or she saw an opportunity to off him and blame it on Tess."

"If that was the plan, it makes it look like the killer could be in the band or at least in his inner circle." I push the button to release my seat belt. It makes a zipping sound as it snaps into its holder next to the car door. "Unless someone else arranged it. Who on the committee worked with the band to arrange the housing?" I ask.

"That was Gina Paris," Jenna says. "I'll talk to her and see what went down when they were finalizing the accommodations. All I know is that we had planned on booking rooms at the Hemlock Inn until the special request came through for a house." Jenna shivers and rubs her palms over her arms. "What a shame. This place would've made a great reception venue. Now it just feels haunted."

I shake my head. "I hope you won't put those thoughts into Tess's head. Otherwise, you'll end up with a permanent roommate because she won't want to go back to her place."

"It might not be a bad idea if we stick together," Jenna says as she and I get out of the car.

I stop and put a hand on her arm before we ascend the porch steps. "This really has shaken you up, hasn't it?"

She bites her bottom lip and nods. That's when I see the anguish in my daughter's pretty face.

"Hey, it's going to be okay," I say. "We're going to get to the bottom of who did this. And if we don't, Jack will."

I give her arm a gentle squeeze, and she takes a deep breath.

"I know," she says. "I think I'm just tired."

"I'll bet you are. Everything seems worse when you're exhausted. Let's finish here so you can get back and take a power nap before the festival starts."

"As if I'd be able to sleep," she says as we start up the porch's concrete steps. "I'll probably just push through and then sleep for about a month after everything is over… after the festival is done and Allan's killer is behind bars."

A shuffling noise from the side of the wraparound porch startles us.

Jenna and I exchange a glance.

"Hello?" I say.

A tall, thin guy with long, dark hair steps into view. Even with the ten feet or so of distance between us, I can see that his eyes and nose are red. Has he been crying?

"Can I help you?" he says.

"Hi, I'm Jenna Bell. I'm the chair of the Hemlock League Ladies Society Harvest Moon Festival. You're Nick Park, aren't you?"

Unsmiling, the guy nods.

I am in awe of my daughter's ability to remember names and present a professional front even when she isn't feeling her best.

"I've come out to check on you and your bandmates," she continues. "I'm so sorry about Allan. Do you all need anything, or can we do anything for you?"

Unblinking, he stares at her for a long moment, long enough for me to wonder if his red eyes are a sign that he's high. But then a tear rolls out of the corner of his right eye. He looks upward at the porch's light blue ceiling, swipes away the tear, and shrugs.

"Thanks, but I don't think there's anything anyone can do. Unless you can call off the cops and make them let us go. I want to get as far away from this place as I can."

Jenna ventures a couple of steps closer to Nick. "I know this is hard for you. I'm so sorry. The police are doing their best to find Allan's killer, and I'm sure they appreciate your cooperation."

With that, Nick lets go of any pretense of keeping a stiff upper lip. The floodgates open and he blubbers like a baby.

"Oh, hey, oh my gosh, I'm so sorry," Jenna says. She glances at me, and we each take a hold of one of Nick's arms. He allows us to walk him to the porch swing, where he sits, hangs his head, and sobs.

Jenna sits next to him, patting his limp hand resting in his lap. I riffle though my purse and find a small package of tissues and hand them to Jenna while I pull over one of the wicker chairs.

"Are you sure you want to play the festival tonight?" I ask.

"It would be perfectly understandable if you decided not to," Jenna says. "I'm sure this has been a crushing shock to you and the band."

Nick sniffs and swipes at his nose.

"Not my decision," he says, and that seems to help him get his bearings, because his demeanor hardens. He takes a deep breath and scowls. "Turns out, this band isn't a democracy."

"What do you mean?" I ask.

"None of us want to play tonight—except for Titania. It's her chance to sing, and she's not letting her big break get away."

"So, no one else in the band except Titania wants to go on tonight?" Jenna asks.

"I don't know." Nick shrugs.

"But you just said no one else wants to go on," Jenna urges gently.

"That's the way it started," Nick says. "I think it's a *hello-fa* disrespect to Allan, but let me just say, Titania can be very persuasive."

"You say that like it's a bad thing." The screen door opens, and Titania steps out onto the porch as if we'd conjured her. "Nick, we agreed that we need the money. If we don't play, we don't get paid. It's that simple."

Her pale skin looks almost translucent. Her platinum blonde hair looks like gossamer, and her diminutive stature and large green eyes, which turn up at the outer corners, give her the appearance of a fairy.

Of course, in lore, fairies can be good or evil. In which camp does Titania live?

She kneels in front of Nick and places her small hand on his knee. "You know Allan would've wanted it this way. He'd hate it if we sat around grieving. It's our duty to keep the band going. That's why the show needs to go on tonight."

Her voice is soft and soothing, and judging by the way Nick's face softens, her words—or maybe it is the way she is stroking his thigh—are having a positive effect on him. It is almost as if she's casting a spell over him. "You know I'm right. Now, go inside and get yourself together. If you can't do it for Allan, do it for me, Nick. Okay?"

Nick gets up and goes inside, exactly as he was told.

The three of us are alone, and Titania's ethereal demeanor hardens. "What can I do for you ladies?" she asks, hands on her hips and her head tilted upward defiantly.

"Titania, we're so sorry for your loss," I say. "I know this has to be a hard time for you and the band. We came to offer our support. Do you need anything?"

She shifts her weight from one boot-clad foot to another and crosses her arms over her chest.

"Yeah, well, it does pretty much suck," she says. "But what can you do?"

"That's a good question," Jenna replies. "We do want to help. I want to reassure you that you and the band don't have to perform tonight if it's too much too soon."

Titania scoffs. "We've already had this conversation. The band wants to play. Nothing has changed. Got it?"

"I'm sorry, but Nick did not seem like he is in any shape to go on stage tonight."

"Yeah, well, I think you need to butt out. We're being paid to do a job, and we will do that job like the professionals we are."

"I have a question," I say.

Titania raises her eyebrows, but her eyes look guarded. "Yes?"

"If you're short a lead singer, who is going to step into that role on such short notice?"

"I'm singing tonight." She says the words like she is covering a shift for a colleague at a fast-food restaurant. "Do you have a problem with that?"

"Of course not," I say. "Can you tell me where you were last night after the gala?"

The petite woman's face twists into a mask of rage. "I don't have to tell you anything. I mean, what business is it of yours?"

"Titania, why are you being so defensive?" Jenna asks.

"Why are you being so intrusive?" she fires back.

"We came out to make sure the band is okay," Jenna says. "I'd hardly call that intrusive. As the chair of the festival, it's my duty to ensure we get what we paid for."

"Oh, I see," she says. "This isn't really a condolence call. You came out to protect your investment."

"I'm sorry," Jenna says. "I didn't mean it that way. What happened to Allan is such a terrible tragedy. I am concerned about you and your bandmates. I do want to make sure you're all okay."

"Well, questioning me like you're the police or you have some kind of authority is hardly making me feel okay—as you put it."

I know the strong words go against my sweet daughter's grain. It isn't in her nature to play hardball in a situation like this, but she's trying to crack this tough nut for Tess's sake. Is Titania really this callous and spotlight hungry, or is this the way she deals with grief? Lord knows we all grieve differently and in ways that don't make sense to other people. I'd be the first to attest to that.

"The contract we signed says the band ShakesPierre would perform at your gala and festival, and that's exactly what we will deliver," Titania says. "Nowhere does it stipulate specific band members will play or sing. We will give you what you paid for, and then we will be on our way. In the meantime, I'd appreciate it if you'd direct all questions to our manager."

"Titania? What's going on?" a tall woman with dark hair opens the screen door and joins us on the porch.

"We were just discussing tonight's performance." Titania glares at Jenna as if challenging her to dispute it. The malice that radiates from Titania's eyes makes me shiver. It's one thing to put on a show-must-go-on front, but it is quite another to project such anger.

And to refuse to tell Jenna where she was last night after the gala.

Is she hiding something?

"Hello, ladies," the woman says and extends a hand to me. "I'm Angel Ferguson, the band manager. Jenna and I know each other, but I believe we haven't met."

After I introduce myself, Angel says, "Will you please excuse us for a moment? Titania, a word, please?"

The tiny woman sighs, but she complies. The two disappear inside the house, leaving Jenna and me alone.

"That was… interesting," Jenna whispers. "What do you make of it?"

Before I can answer, we hear the sound of muffled arguing and a crash. Both of us get to our feet and start toward the screen door, but Angel heads us off and steps outside onto the porch again.

"Please excuse Titania. We're all a little emotional today. I'm sure you understand."

"Absolutely, but is everything okay in there?" I point toward the door.

"What do you mean?" Angel asks.

"We heard something that sounded like a crash," Jenna says.

Angel smiles. "Oh, that. Titania dropped a glass. I would invite you in, but she's in the middle of cleaning it up. I'd hate for anyone to get hurt."

The irony of her word hangs in the air between us.

Angel's mouth forms a perfect "o," and she waves away the words. "What I meant was, I'd hate for anyone to cut themselves on a piece of glass."

This morning, Angel is dressed in a stylish, trim black suit with a white silk scoop-neck blouse. The outfit is suitable for mourning... or the rock and roll business.

"Of course," Jenna says. "I knew what you meant."

"Angel, if you have a moment, we'd like to ask you some questions," I say. "We won't take too much time because we all need to get ready for the festival. But—"

"I can assure you that everyone in the band is prepared to give you a wonderful show tonight. Please don't worry." She smiles again, beatifically, like a patient Madonna indulging the ignorant.

"Actually, Titania already assured us of that," I say. "So that's not what we wanted to talk to you about."

Angel's smile falters. She lowers herself onto the wicker chair where I sat when we were comforting Nick.

"Did the band leave the gala together last night?" I ask.

Angel purses her lips and stares off into the middle distance. "The guys and I took the bus back to the house. I had a blinding headache and decided to call it an early night. Well, earlier than usual."

"What about the guys?" Jenna asks.

Angel falters. "All the guys except for Allan and—" She stops and bites her bottom lip.

"Titania?" I prompt.

Angel nods. "She and Allan said they were going to the bar for a drink. They were going to Uber it back to the house. I think I heard them come in sometime around 2:30 a.m. ... or maybe it was 3:30 or 4:00 a.m. I can't be sure."

"You said you heard them come in," I ask. "Did you specifically hear Allan?"

"No, I can't tell you who it was because I was so groggy. I remember stirring when I heard whoever it was come in the front door. I did get up to go to the bathroom at 4:00. I know that for sure because I looked at the clock to see how much time I had left to sleep. So, whoever came in was in by that time."

"The police arrived at the murder scene sometime after 4:17 a.m."

Angel draws in a sharp breath. "I guess that means when I got up, Allan was… gone—" A sob escapes and she corners her mouth. "To think, I had no idea what had happened to him. I can assure you I want to do everything I can to help find who did this. Please, tell me what you need."

"One thing that would help is if we could get a copy of Titania's ride receipt. It should be stored within the app on her phone, shouldn't it?"

"I'll ask her." Angel scrunches up her face. "But maybe not right now. She puts up a tough front, but she's taking this pretty hard. I hope you understand."

Even if we couldn't get a copy of the receipt from Titania, not many Uber drivers in Hemlock worked at that hour. It wouldn't be hard to find out who picked her up and brought her home. Depending on Allan's official time of death, the driver could either serve as an alibi for Titania or further muddy the waters about her innocence.

My first inclination is to call Jack to compare notes, to

see if he knew about this, but he and I are still at odds—or, more aptly, I am still at odds... with life.

He was quite cordial this morning. Even if he has met someone else—the blond at the gala last night—in the short time we'd been apart, we could still be friends. Maybe it's time I extend an olive branch.

"Do you know of anyone who might have wanted Allan dead?" Jenna asks.

Her hand flutters to the neckline of her blouse, and she closes her eyes.

When she reopens them, they are shiny with tears.

"This is so hard—" Her voice breaks on the last word. "Much more difficult than I could've ever imagined. But then again, who would even imagine something like this?" She shakes her head as if clearing it. "The police were here all morning asking these questions. I don't mind talking to you, but do you mind if I ask why you're here?"

Jenna and I glance at each other.

"Tess has been implicated in Allan's murder, and I know she's innocent. We are determined to get to the bottom of it. Will you help us? Please?"

Angel's face falls. "I'm so sorry. Things seem to be going from bad to worse, don't they? Tess is so sweet. I can't imagine that she would be capable of murder. I mean, despite the bad blood between her and Allan."

The pregnant pause makes me realize exactly how bad this looks for Tess.

"But you know I love Tess," Angel continues. "I'm happy to help in any way I can if it will help clear her. And even more important, I want to the cops to find the person who did this to Allan." She sighs. "I wish I could give you more information, but I have to say—and I told this to the police—I don't know of anyone who wanted Allan dead."

"What about the band members?" I ask.

Angel shook her head. "We're a close group. We all get along so well."

Jenna and I both shoot her a look. I don't believe that statement one bit.

"Well, I mean, when a group of people work, live, and travel together, there are bound to be days when we want to kill each other—figuratively speaking, of course—and they're artists, so they have their temperamental moments. But when it comes down to it, we are like family. We love like family, we fight like a family, and we protect each other like family—" She chokes on the words and sobs.

"I'm sorry. It hits me in waves. One minute I'm sitting here talking to you like a good business manager would, and then it like, oh, man, Allan is gone. He's *dead* and we're never going to see him again."

She buries her face in her hands for a moment. When she looks up, I hand her a tissue from the packet I offered Nick earlier. She accepts it and blows her nose.

"This just doesn't seem real," she says.

"I know it doesn't," says Jenna. "And I know this isn't

easy for you, but I just have a couple more questions."

Angel nods and blots the edges of her eyes. "Sure."

"Whose idea was it to stay in a house rather than a hotel?"

She squints like she doesn't understand the question and shrugs.

"If we're staying somewhere for more than a night, we always prefer to get a house rather than a hotel. It gives us a chance to stretch out. And with the availability of short-term vacation rentals, houses are always a possibility."

I make a mental note to check where the band stayed the last time it was on the road. If worse comes to worst, I can ask Jack to ask Angel for specifics. If he hasn't thought of this line of questioning already, it is a viable one.

"Why choose a house so far off the beaten path?" Jenna asks.

Angel laughs. "This is a band. They can be loud and boisterous. Neighbors tend to complain when the guys decide to jam in the wee hours of the morning."

The three of us sit quietly, listening to the silence. "They're not being very loud today," I say.

"That's because some of them are sleeping and others, like Titania, are probably already starting to get ready for the show tonight."

I glance at my watch. "It's only 1:30. The show doesn't start until 7:00."

Angel tucks a piece of hair behind her ear. "Until you get

the chance to sing lead vocals for a crowd, you probably won't understand the urgency."

"Is this the first time Titania will take the spotlight?"

"It is her first time singing alone." There is something in Angel's expression, the flash of something almost imperceptible in her eyes that betrays her otherwise calm exterior.

"So, Allan dies, and she gets to go on solo," I say, opting to step in as the bad cop to Jenna's more congenial role.

Angel frowns at me, then opens her mouth as if to say something but stops short. She clears her throat and then continues. "I'm not sure what you're implying, but Titania is taking one for the team by stepping up to the microphone tonight. I'm sure it's not an easy thing for her."

"That's not what it sounded like when she and Nick were out here earlier," I say.

Angel stands abruptly. "Excuse me, what exactly are you implying?"

"I'm not implying anything, but I am asking you if Titania would kill Allan for her own shot at fame?"

Chapter Eight

~ Jenna ~

THIS ISN'T THE first time my mother and I have been asked to leave a place after we asked hard questions during an investigation. But it's okay. We need to get to the park where the crews are setting up for the festival. I need to check in with my committee chairs and make sure all is well.

I can't blame Angel for being protective of Titania. Angel has an alibi—she went back to the house on the bus with the rest of the band—but Titania's is this Uber driver we still need to find. My gut is telling me her story may not add up. Does Angel know that and is covering for her? Because if the spare singer goes down, the band will be out of commission until they can find a replacement—if they do find a replacement—and Angel will be out of a job.

At the park, which is located in the center of downtown Hemlock, the stage for tonight's performance is set up at the south end, and the food booths are scattered along the west side of the park. The crisp, fall air smells of fresh cut hay and mulled apple cider steeping ahead of tonight's festivities. We are expecting the crowds to start gathering around 5:00 p.m.

I greet several of the committee members and stop for quick updates before I spy Tess talking to one of the vendors who had rented a booth to sell caramel apples. I make my way over to join them.

She introduces me to Barry Blenheim, and we exchange pleasantries. I sidestep questions about Allan's murder, news of which has apparently made it to the press. Huh, the tragedy might entice the curious to come out tonight. I make a mental note to talk to Jack about the possibility for police presence. For the thrill seekers—not to mention that a murderer is still on the loose.

When Barry turns away to adjust the sign hanging on his booth, I ask Tess, "How are you?"

She forces a smile and lifts her chin. "I'm fine."

"Everything looks great, Barry," she calls to the man. "Let me know if you need anything."

Tess motions with her head for me to follow her. When we are out of earshot of other people, she says, "I let Jack fingerprint me."

"Should you have done that?" I ask.

"Why wouldn't I?" she says. "I have nothing to hide."

"I was just wondering if we should've talked to Ian before you did that."

"Jenna, I'm not under arrest. And my cooperating with the fingerprinting process will allow them to rule me out as a suspect. That will be one less person on their list."

I bite my bottom lip. "Did Jack show you the murder weapon? Was the knife yours?"

She shakes her head. "No, it had already been submitted for evidence. I may be a chef, but I'm not the only person in this town who owns a knife. Besides, none of mine are missing. I just feel so bad for Allan I mean, we had our differences, and he could be a real peace of work, but he didn't deserve this. I just can't stop wondering who he angered enough to make it come to this."

"I suppose that's the million-dollar question," I say.

I tell Tess about our visit to the farmhouse where the band is staying. "I suppose you've heard they're insisting that the show will go on, right?"

"I hadn't heard," she says. "Not officially, anyway. But I guess I'm kind of surprised. I don't know if I could do it. It's going to take all I have to get through what I have to do tonight, and I don't have to get up on stage."

She grimaces. "Well, I don't have to get up there now, anyway. Will you refund the money to the high bidder of my duet with Allan?"

"Mary and Steve Crawford had the winning bid," I said. "They're letting us keep the $500 since it benefits the library."

"That's nice of them," Tess says.

"It is. But I have more news. The plot is getting even more interesting." I fill her in on how Titania is set to go on solo, and why her alibi seems a little questionable. "I should've asked Angel if Titania will be the solo front person going forward. Though it's probably too early for them to know what the future holds."

"Titania would bring a totally different sound to the band," Tess says.

I nod. "I don't know that blind ambition to be the lone lead singer of a band like ShakesPierre necessarily implicates her, but we do need to track down that Uber driver and see if he can give us a solid time frame of when he picked her up and dropped her off at the house."

"Look, here comes Jack," Tess says. "If you haven't already, maybe you can tell him what you've learned and see if he knows anything."

We both wave at Jack as he approaches. He looks grim.

"How's it going?" I say. "I have some information about the Allan Bossert case that you might find useful."

Jack's brow furrows. "I'd love to hear what you have to say, Jenna, but right now, I'm here on a more pressing matter."

He directs his attention to Tess. "I'm sorry. I don't want to do this, but I don't have a choice. Tess Harrison, I'm placing you under arrest in the murder of Allan Bossert. After Allan's stunt at the gala last night, you have a well-documented motive—"

"But, Jack, did the guy embarrass me? Sure," Tess says. "Would I kill him over it? No way."

"Even so, the prints on the murder weapon—a chef's

knife—came back a match," he says. "Your fingerprints were all over it, Tess.

"You have the right to remain silent. Anything you say can and will be used against you in a court of law. You have the right to an attorney. If you cannot afford an attorney, one will be provided for you. Do you understand the rights I have just read to you?"

Tess does something that looks like a half shrug, half nod. "But, Jack, I didn't do it."

"I want to believe you, but the knife came back with your prints. I wish you could give me some sort of proof of your innocence—like an alibi I can check out."

"Jack, I live alone," she says. "I told you, I went straight home from the gala. I got there around 1:30 a.m., and Allan showed up at my door around 3:00 a.m. We talked for about ten minutes and then he left. I didn't even let him inside."

"What did you talk about?" Jack asks.

"Tess, stop." I stick my hand out between them like a traffic cop. "Don't say anything else without talking to an attorney."

"I've already answered all of his questions when I went in earlier to be *voluntarily* fingerprinted."

"Have you considered the attack might have been a random mugging?" I ask. "Allan was walking by himself in the early hours of the morning."

"Why would we find a chef's knife with the chef's fingerprints on it not far from the scene of the crime?" Jack points out. "There's never been a mugging in downtown Hemlock. Besides, his wallet was in his pocket. He was still wearing a diamond-studded watch on his wrist, and he had at least four karats of ice in his ears. If it was a mugging, that's what they would've gone for."

"I don't care," I say. "This is never going to hold up in court."

Jack frowns. "We've got the evidence and motive, Jenna. I'm sorry."

Tess sighs on an exhale and stands there looking absolutely defeated, like all her fight and resilience left on the breath she blew out.

Is it any wonder? She's endured so much in the last twenty-four hours: the indignity of being bullied by Pierre—or Allan or whatever his name was—no disrespect to the dead, but come on, the guy had been insufferable—then finding him dead right next to her bakery and going down to the station to be fingerprinted all in the name of cooperation. Now she is being arrested.

It's all proof positive that no good deed goes unpunished.

It is a lot. And, I have to admit, none of it looks good.

I am worried Tess will slip back into the shock she'd suffered this morning when I found her sitting in the police car giving a statement.

"Jack, please don't handcuff her," I say. "She's not resisting arrest, and you know Tess. You know she won't run."

Jack looks me in the eyes for the first time, and he looks

absolutely stricken. It hurts my heart almost as much as seeing Tess standing there shrinking into herself.

He nods almost imperceptibly. "Come with me, Tess. I have to take you into the station."

"Wait," I say. "Tess, where is your purse?"

"It's in the trunk of my car. I'm parked in the city lot because I wasn't ready to go home... after everything. Someone will need to move my car before morning so it doesn't get towed."

"I'll do that, and I'll get your purse for you."

"No," Jack says. "You have to stay away from the car until my men can search it and write a report."

"But her purse is in there," I say.

"She won't need her purse," Jack says tersely. "We already got her information when we fingerprinted her. She won't be able to have it with her in the holding cell. I'd just have to check it in with her belongings. But I will need her keys so I can get into the car. Where are they?"

"They're in the right hip pocket of my jeans." Tess keeps her hands at her sides and makes no attempt to reach for it.

I know she is being cautious. So far, Jack hasn't cuffed her, and I am sure she doesn't want to make any sudden moves that might give him reason to think he needs to. Even though there is no way she has a gun or another weapon in the front pocket of her skinny jeans.

I hold my hands out in front of me, palms out. "Jack, I am going to reach into Tess's pocket and get her keys. Are you okay with that?"

He sighs, looking a bit exasperated. "Just do it."

"Can she take my phone?" Tess asks as I pull out her keys. "It's in my back pocket."

"I'll need to take it in," Jack says. "It will be entered into evidence."

"Um… okay. I don't know what you think you're going to find." She keeps her hands at her sides. "May I turn around so Jenna can get it out of my back pocket?"

"No, you stay right where you are. Do not move."

"Wow, Jack, way to treat her like the criminal you know she's not."

Something—a look of remorse, maybe—flashes in Jack's eyes before they shutter and the cop in him takes over. "If I were treating her like a criminal, I would slap handcuffs on her, and if you keep it up, I will."

"I'm sorry," I murmur. "I shouldn't have said that."

He frowns. Without a doubt, his tough guy act is a cover for how much he hates having to do this.

He holds out his hand, and I give him Tess's keys.

"I'm going to walk around and get her cell phone out of her back pocket," I say. "Is that okay?"

Jack gives a curt nod. "Hurry up."

I glance around to assess if anyone in the park has twigged to what is going on. So far, everyone seems to be unaware and going about their business. I have to give Jack credit for handling this so discreetly. He doesn't even have backup, which would surely draw a significant amount of attention. Right now, to those who know us, it probably just looks like the two cochairs of the festival talking to the chief of police.

It doesn't matter what those who don't know us thinks... or at least that's what I told myself.

Though, it probably looks weird that I am pulling things out of Tess's pockets while she stands there with her arms at her sides.

Her hands are trembling and it makes my heart hurt.

I offer Jack her phone, and he takes it. "What's the passcode?"

Tess tells him. He tries it out and then jots it down in his notebook.

"What are you going to do with the car after your officers search it?" I ask.

"After we're done with it, you're free to move it so it doesn't get towed."

"Will you authorize your team to give me the keys after they're finished?"

"If I have Tess's permission," he says.

She nods. "Of course."

"Tess, do you need me to take care of anything else?" I ask as she walks, unhandcuffed, toward the patrol car with Jack.

"Bella," she says. "Will you please feed Bella and change her litter box?"

Bella is Tess's gray and white pound kitty. She rescued her from the Hemlock Animal Shelter, and Bella has been Tess's baby since day one.

"She'll be in good hands. Don't worry, okay? I will take care of everything. I'll call Ian, and he will get you out. Most importantly, remember, it is your right to remain silent. They can only hold you for seventy-two hours without charging you. Do not say a word until you have a chance to talk to Ian."

What I don't tell Tess is that the seventy-two hours does not include weekends, and today is Saturday.

Chapter Nine

~ Maddie ~

I GET TO the park just in time to see Tess getting into the back of Jack's patrol car. Jenna looks horrified and helpless as she watches Jack close the door.

"What's going on?" I ask.

"Jack just arrested Tess in the Allan Bossert murder case." Jenna's voice shakes.

The reality of it pierces my heart. My hand flies to my chest because I really feel a physical pain.

I am opening my mouth to ask her for the details when I notice a small group of people—nobody I recognize, which means they aren't local—has stopped to watch the activity. It is likely that they're fans who heard about the murder and came to see what they could see.

The group is far enough away that they couldn't have heard Jenna. Since Tess isn't cuffed and Jack hasn't used his lights or siren, thank goodness, they really didn't get much of a show. It simply looks like someone is riding away in the back seat of a patrol car.

As if anyone does that by choice.

The people look at Jenna and me as if they are expecting us to give them the scoop.

So I do what anyone who wants to throw someone off the scent would do—I smile and wave at the car as it pulls away.

Jenna leans in and asks in a low voice, "What in the world are you doing?"

Keeping the smile plastered to my face, I whisper, "I'm trying to confuse some lookie-loos."

Jenna's gaze darts in the direction of the bystanders. She turns around so her back is to them and she, too, waves in the direction of the vanishing car. "I see. Let's move along."

As we walk farther down the sidewalk that parallels the park, away from the curious bystanders, I'm finally able to ask her, "What in the world is going on?"

Jenna gives me the point by point of what had transpired in the park.

"This can't be happening," I say.

"I know," Jenna agrees. "I need to call Ian. The conference he's attending should be winding down in a few hours. He's supposed to be home tomorrow, but maybe he can talk to Tess over the phone, or, better yet, maybe he can get an earlier flight."

Jenna sits on one of the park benches along the side wall and calls Ian. My rational side doesn't want to be upset with Jack. He's just doing his job. But when you see your daughter's best friend, a young woman who is like your own daughter, being hauled off to the police station, it's hard to be rational.

Not to mention that Jack didn't even look at me. He just got in his car and drove away. Although, since I had just walked up, there's a possibility that he hadn't seen me standing there.

Yeah, maybe if he were blind.

I want to believe that he was embarrassed to arrest Tess. But I can't shake the feeling that his reaction is his way of putting up a wall and signaling to me that this case isn't open for discussion.

With the other two murders in Hemlock, he's made it clear that it goes against protocol to talk about active cases. Yet I've always managed to respect his position while getting him to talk about leads by speaking in hypotheticals or paralleling the case to one in one of my cozy mystery manuscripts. We've done this even when Jenna had been a person of interest in her ex-boyfriend's murder and when, for a hot minute in July, I had been on the suspect list when my former writing critique partner, Kellen Corsi, had been killed when she returned for a reunion weekend.

Clearly, he is making a point that there will be no discussion about Tess's case—hypothetical or under the guise of research.

Yeah, well, we'll see about that.

Jenna ends her call with Ian. "He's going to call Tess at

the police station and then catch a flight home tonight."

"I'm so glad to hear that."

"I just don't get it," Jenna says. "Tess told me that all her knives were in her knife case when she left the gala last night. That's why she went in voluntarily to be fingerprinted this morning. I mean, if she'd killed Allan—which she didn't because Tess is not capable of something so heinous, but let's just pretend for a minute that she did do it—do you really think she would she go in and voluntarily hand them the proof they needed to arrest her? Mom, I think someone is setting her up."

"It sure looks that way," I say. "But did she check to make sure all the knives were still there this morning?"

"Well, I'm not sure. She didn't say, but I doubt it. She did say that after the gala she let herself into the shop to put away some of the things she had used in the kitchen during the gala. She didn't mention whether her knives were part of that gear, but those knives are so expensive you know she didn't leave them in the Briar Patch kitchen overnight, especially since she was going to be tied up with the festival today.

"Then, she said after she got back up to the apartment, Allan knocked on her door. We know she didn't let him in. She talked to him outside. She hasn't been back to the apartment since discovering his body and talking to the police."

Jenna and I exchange a knowing look.

"The police are going to search Tess's car," Jenna says. "Jack is going to instruct the officers to give the keys to me so I can move her car out of the parking lot."

"So, if you have her car keys, it probably means that you'll have her house key, too."

Jenna nods. "I told her I would take care of Bella while she's... dealing with this."

"When we move Tess's car from the city lot into her space at her apartment, we will just go up and take care of sweet Bella," I say. "While we're there, we might as well have a look for ourselves."

Chapter Ten

~ *Jenna* ~

AFTER THE OFFICERS release Tess's keys to me, we do a drive-by to see if the police are still nosing around The Briar Patch and Tessa's apartment.

When she drove to my apartment to get some sleep after the voluntary fingerprinting, she hadn't been considered a suspect, so the police haven't made her apartment part of the crime scene. But now that they have searched her car, if they haven't searched her apartment, surely that's coming soon.

Boy, that will give Janey Powers something to talk about. I just hope the officers will be as discreet about it as Jack has been about the arrest. But cops are cops, and they don't have a personal relationship with Tess, so who knows what will happen.

Returning her car to her parking space after it's been gone most of the day will at least make things appear to be normal.

We don't say much as we drive to Tessa's apartment. Honestly, I think we are both holding our breaths because we are unsure of what we might find. We both breathe a huge sigh of relief when we arrive and see that the police have packed up and gone.

The only evidence that something nefarious has happened is the alleyway is still cordoned off with crime scene tape, but we don't need the alleyway to access Tess's apartment, which is directly above the bakery. The entrance to her home is in the back.

"I wonder if Jack's crew has searched Tessa's apartment?" I muse. "When he came to arrest Tess, everything happened so fast—and he was not very talkative, as you can imagine—we didn't get a chance to ask him. But as he did with moving the car, he didn't specifically tell me to stay away. Is that odd? It seems kind of odd to me."

"Well, I'd be surprised if they haven't already searched her place. Though it does take time to get a warrant. But they found the body in the alley. From what I understand, there was no immediate sign that Allan had been moved to the alley from somewhere else. So the apartment and the bakery aren't really the crime scene, which is probably why they don't have it cordoned off. The Hemlock Police Department has its hands full today with the possibility of Allan's murder attracting larger crowd than usual to the festival, but we still need to get in and out of there as quickly as possible."

I turn off of Main Street onto Catalpa Avenue and make a quick right turn onto Acorn Street, which runs behind the building. Both the street and Tess's designated parking spot are empty. I steer the car into her space and kill the engine.

Mom and I don't waste time lingering. I pop the trunk and we make our way up the steps to her apartment.

It is eerily quiet, except for the distant sounds coming from the park where the ShakesPierre road crew is testing its sound system. As we stand on the landing in front of Tess's front door, we can look down and see the alleyway where the murder happened.

Except for the crime scene tape, it looks normal. So normal, it makes me shiver.

"If you didn't know what happened down there, you'd never dream that's where a man lost his life."

My mom nods. "Who wanted you dead, Allan?"

I slide the key into the lock and open the door. "You're right. This wasn't a random mugging. Who did it? Why did they do it in Hemlock, and why did they frame Tess?"

I shut the door behind me, and for a moment, Mom and I stand in the living room of Tess's small apartment, the calm settling around us. The only sound now is the ambient hum of the refrigerator. Muted light filters in through the only window in the room, which looks out over the dreaded crime scene alleyway. The place smells like it always does, of baking spices—cinnamon, cloves, and nutmeg—and apples.

But I know my tenderhearted best friend well enough to know that from now on, she will have a hard time thinking of anything but the murder when she is in this apartment.

As I move to set Tess's purse on the coffee table, I see a flash of movement out of the corner of my eye. My hand flies to my mouth as I try to stifle a startled scream. White-hot pin pricks of panic threaten to paralyze me until Bella lands with a thud and saunters over to wind figure eights around my legs.

Both my mother and I shrink a little as we exhale our relief.

"Oh, my gosh," Mom says. "I thought someone was in here."

"I know," I agree. "Bella, where did you come from? You scared us to death, you rotten cat."

As I squat down to give her a few strokes, I glance up and realize she had probably been hiding on the bookshelf just inside Tess's front door and jumped down to greet us.

"Since I'll need to feed Bella while Tess is… away…" I can't bring myself to say the words *under arrest* or *in jail*, even though they are bouncing around my mind like ping-pong balls in a storm. "I'm going to take her to my house to make sure she doesn't get out if the police do search the place. After all Tess has been through, the last thing she needs is for Bella to get lost."

"That's a good idea," my mom says. "We will need to round up her litter box and her food. Do you know if there is a carrier for us to transport her?"

"I'm sure there is. We can keep an eye out as we have a look around. How about I have a nose around the kitchen.

Do you want to take the bedroom?"

"Sure. You look for her knives, and I'll look check to see if anything seems amiss."

In true Tess fashion, her kitchen—her whole apartment, for that matter—is neat as a pin. That is the thing about my friend, she never needs to worry about the condition of her home if anyone pops in unexpectedly. I am not so lucky. My bed is unmade and my boxers and T-shirt are on the bathroom floor where I left them after getting Tess's call. Granted, Tess had been leaving for work and I had been startled awake out of a sound sleep, but I've always known I could learn a thing or two from my best friend.

A sweeping glance around the compact kitchen doesn't reveal the canvas and leather roll-up bag that holds her knives, so I began opening cabinet doors and drawers... even the small pantry and refrigerator. All to no avail.

The knives aren't here.

I could kick myself for not asking her where she left them, but then again, she doesn't need to be talking about anything in front of Jack until she's had a chance to consult with Ian.

On an impulse, I pull out my phone and text him.

Me: *When you talk to Tess, please ask her where she left the carrier bag she uses to transport her knives.*

He doesn't answer. I hope that means he was on his way to the airport or at least in the process of changing his flight.

As I slide my phone into my back pocket, my mother

comes into the kitchen.

"Nothing seems out of the ordinary," she says. "And I found the cat carrier. It's in the hall closet. Rather than emptying and cleaning Bella's litter box, why don't we buy a new one? We can stop by the hardware store. They have a pet section. While you're finishing up in here, I'll go have a look around the living room."

There isn't much left to look through in the kitchen, though I do go back through the drawers to see if Tess has a spare set of chef's knives. I find steak knives, but no cooking knives. Tess takes pride in using only the best tools. When business at the Briar Patch started picking up about a year after she opened it, one of the first things she purchased was a set of quality chef's knives. She took her old set down to the bakery's kitchen for her staff to use—

Whoa. Wait a minute. If the knife the murderer used to kill Allan isn't from Tess's personal selection, it might have been taken from the Briar Patch kitchen.

We need to let ourselves into the bakery and have a look around. The key is bound to be on the set Tess gave to me this afternoon. I have no idea how many extra knives she keeps in her commercial kitchen—in fact, would Tess even know—but I still need to go down there and have a look around. I'm opening my mouth to tell my mom when she says, "Hey, Jenna. Quick, come in here. Look at this."

I step into the living room, and she's standing at the window looking down on the crime scene.

She motions me over but doesn't take her eyes off whatever it is she's looking at.

"What is it?" I ask. I look out and spot exactly what has given her pause. A tall, thin guy wearing black-rimmed hipster sunglasses and a white T-shirt with the ShakesPierre band members emblazoned on the front of it. He is standing at the crime scene tape stretched across the entrance to the alley that opens onto the street where we parked Tess's car—not the side that opens onto Main Street.

He looks around as if assessing the situation—probably checking to see if anyone is nearby—and a moment later, he ducks under the tape and walks into the alley.

"He has just breached the crime scene line," I say, as if my mother isn't seeing the same thing. "What should we do?"

"I think we need to watch him and see what he does," she says. "Do you recognize him?"

"I've never seen him in my life," I say.

He looks several years younger than me. So I wouldn't have gone to school with him, but one of the perks—and curses—of living in a small town like Hemlock is that everyone knows everyone. This guy isn't from around here.

That doesn't mean he isn't from the college in Brevard, which is only a few miles away. Or, maybe more obviously, he's a fan of the band and came to town for tonight's concert. But what is he doing nosing around the crime scene?

Word about Allan Bossert's death has gotten out, but if I know Jack as well as I think I do, since it's an active investigation, he hasn't released details of the murder. The only people who knew that this is the scene are those who were around last night… or, technically, early this morning.

Would news like this travel that fast? Or does this guy, whoever he is, know more than any run-of-the-mill fan should know? I pull out my phone and zoom in on him the best I can to get a photo before he wanders out of range.

I snap a couple of shots before the guy bends down, picks up something, and shoves it into his pocket.

"Did you see that?" I ask.

My mom nods. "He picked up something, but I couldn't tell what it was."

I have a photo of him, but even though I expand the shot as much as possible, I can't see what he was reaching for.

"I was going to suggest that we let ourselves into the bakery to see if Tess's knives are in the kitchen and do an inventory of extra knives, but this guy gives me the creeps," I say. "If he is brazen enough to cross a police line, who knows what else he would do… or has already done."

"I think we need to call Jack and report him," Mom says.

"Really? You mean after we leave?"

"No, I mean now. As much as I'd love to go down there and ask the guy some questions myself, I think he will run the minute he knows someone is onto him."

She already has her phone out and is placing the call.

"He crossed the police line. We did not. Tess gave us her keys. She gave us permission to enter her apartment. We are doing nothing wrong—"

I can just make out the sound of Jack answering the call.

"Hi, Maddie," he says.

My mom draws in a breath before saying, "Jack, hi, I'm so glad you picked up," and fills him in on the situation.

When she hangs up, she tells me, "He's on his way. He wants us to stay inside and move away from the window."

Chapter Eleven

~ *Maddie* ~

ABOUT TWENTY MINUTES later, Jack knocks on the door. I know it's him because I can see his bulky frame through the peephole of Tess's front door.

"Maddie," he says.

The sound of his voice unleashes the same butterflies that have taken up residence in my stomach since the first time I met him. But in the early days, much like the past two months, I hadn't allowed myself to call them what they were.

They are a sign that I have feelings for this man. Even if I have no idea what to do with these feelings, they are real. There is no denying them.

"Come in, Jack," I say.

Despite his all-business tone, the look in his eyes is more approachable. It makes me think of the times in the past when I've tried to get him to talk about police work when he really shouldn't, but he's always left the figurative door open just enough that I'm able to finagle it out of him.

He steps inside. Before I realize what I am doing, I

breathe in deeply, inhaling his scent—leather, coffee, aftershave, and soap—those notes that, separately, are so common, but combined, and on him, are intoxicating and stir up the butterflies all over again.

I feel my face heat, so I turn my back to him as I shut the door. I still don't know what I am doing or how I feel. It seems that, just like now, sometimes feelings I have no control over flare up out of nowhere, without rationale or warning, leaving me addled and confused and at a loss for what to say or do.

The inevitable tide of guilt crashes over me.

"There was no one in the alley when my men and I got there," he says. This time his voice is all business. He isn't looking at me anymore, and for a split second I wonder if I imagined the tenderness that had been there when I opened the door.

He walks over to the window.

"Well, you must've missed him." My voice sounds defensive, and I hate that. I clear my throat. "Jenna, show Chief Bradley the photo you took, please."

So much for neutral. The words *Chief Bradley* sound very pointed.

She pulls up the picture and hands him the phone. Jack studies it and nods.

"It's not that I doubted you…" His words trail off. "Will you text it to me, Jenna?"

"Sure," she says as he hands the phone back to her.

As she texts, Jack radios the information to his deputies.

I draw my lips between my teeth; I'm afraid that I might inadvertently blurt out something like, *Who was the blonde you were with last night, Jack?*

The blonde is none of my business.

I didn't return his calls. He has every right to move on. Even if two months is a fast change of heart. Too fast. Much too fast. Did I mean nothing to you, Jack?

And that's just a ridiculous thought because all these years I've been keeping him at arm's length... until I didn't.

Even then it was just a kiss.

"What are you doing up here?" Jack's terse words shake me back from my inner conversation with myself. For the blink of an eye—literally—I'm not sure if he is speaking to Jenna and me or to one of his deputies on the radio.

"There's no reason we shouldn't be here," Jenna says. "We are here legally. Tess gave us her keys."

"After I placed her under arrest," he says.

"And your point is?" I ask.

"My point is, it's a good thing my men searched her place before we arrested her. Otherwise, you would be interfering with an investigation, and I know you wouldn't intentionally do that, would you?"

"Boy, you work fast. But I think you know me well enough to answer that question yourself, Jack," I say before I can stop myself.

His eyes flash. "Well, I thought I knew you, but obviously I was mistaken. Because the woman I thought I was getting involved with wouldn't ghost me."

Jenna clears her throat. "Well, this is substantially awkward. The two of you obviously have things you need to discuss. And, frankly, it's about time. How about if I go back to the park and check on the festival setup and leave you two alone to hash this out?"

"No," Jack and I say together.

"We don't know if that guy who was lurking around the crime scene is out there. You don't need to be down there by yourself."

Jenna's eyes grow large, and I wait for her to tell Jack that she is perfectly capable of taking care of herself.

"Look, Jack," she says in a measured tone. "We're here to pick up Tess's cat. Someone has to care for her while Tess is away. Thank you for taking care not to let Bella out when you and your men searched the place."

Jack nods.

"Also, when you searched the place earlier, was Tess's knife bag here?" she asks.

Jack frowns but doesn't answer.

"Come on, Jack," Jenna says. "I know you can't tell us a lot, but please answer that one question. Tess wasn't cooking today. She was overseeing the food vendors for the festival. The Briar Patch is supposed to have a booth there selling coffee and cookies, which the staff made a couple of days ago and wrapped up to sell. She cherishes those knives. They cost her a lot of hard-earned money. She's super careful with them. Since she wasn't working today, her knife pack would've been in her apartment. She wouldn't even have left them in the bakery's kitchen. If her knives weren't here, that means someone took them. That is another piece of evidence that suggests someone is trying to set her up."

Jack seems to be taking it all in. I can virtually see the wheels in his head turning. Since the temperature between us has cooled, I take a chance. "Jack, please. Just throw us that one little bone of information."

He stares down at his shoes for a moment, then looks back at me. "The knives were here. That's one of the main things we were looking for. We took them in as evidence."

Is that good or not good? I have to recalculate. I guess it means one less reason to think someone is setting up Tess, but maybe the knife didn't come from her pack.

"Were all the knives accounted for?" I ask.

Jack doesn't answer. I can feel in my bones that he won't be so generous with that particular piece of information. So, I change tactics.

"Have you at least asked Tess to identify the murder weapon?"

"Maddie, you know I can't answer any more questions about the investigation. Especially since you and Jenna are emotionally involved."

"I know that, Jack, but if you can't show it to her, Tess could look at a photo and tell you if the knife belongs to her.

If not, maybe she would know if it was one from the bakery's kitchen or even from the kitchen at the Hemlock Inn last night. Knives from either of those places could've had her fingerprints on them. Knowing that, doesn't it sound like someone could've easily gotten ahold of a knife that Tess touched and used it to murder Allan Bossert?"

"Those are all good points," Jack says. "I've considered them all. If you two are finished in here, I am happy to walk you out."

We herd Bella into her carrier and Jack helps us haul her food and scratching post over to Jenna's car, which is parked behind the bridal shop. He doesn't say much as the three of us walk, and I'm not sure if it is because he is on high alert for the kid who crashed the crime scene or if his quietness is of a more personal nature.

However, he lingers after Jenna drives away, and I seize the opportunity.

"Jack, I'm sorry. I didn't mean to hurt you. I haven't been myself since…"

I see his throat work. "I understand that. And I was more than willing to give you some room. What hurts the most is that you couldn't even talk to me as a friend. You just cut me out of your life, Maddie, like you were deadheading a flower."

"And it didn't take long for you to move on, did it?"

I know I have no right to turn things back on him. And, really, that isn't my intention. I just need to know who she is.

Jack looks confused. "I have no idea what you're talking about."

"Are you trying to gaslight me?" An accusatory little laugh escapes before I can stop it. "Because that's really not your style, Jack."

He squints at me. "I truly have no idea what you are talking about."

"The woman from last night, Jack. You brought a date to the gala. The pretty blonde. I saw her with my own eyes."

His mouth falls open for a moment before his lips curve into a smile and a hint of a laugh escapes. "That was my sister, Angela. She's visiting from Orlando. I had that extra ticket to the gala, and I figured I might as well not let it go to waste. I would've introduced you to her if you would have bothered to give me the time of day."

"Your sister?" It takes a moment for the reality to sink in. I've heard of him speak of her, but in the photos I'd seen of her she was a brunette, not a blonde.

"She changed her hair?" I ask.

His brows lift, and, for the first time in a long time, he seems more like himself.

"I would've loved to have met her. I feel like such a fool now. Last night, I thought you'd brought a date and I didn't want to… intrude."

"Were you jealous?"

No. My cheeks burn. I don't quite know what to say.

"Yes. I suppose I was."

He nods, looking satisfied, and just this side of smug. I desperately want him to say something, anything, to break the ice, because I don't quite know how to get from where we were to where I wish we could be. I realize that the ball is probably in my court, but the fact that I can even admit that the ball could be in play is a huge step.

"Jack, please don't give up on me."

His smile makes my toes curl in my boots. "That's all I need to know," he says. "Well, that and I need you to talk to me. Can we start over from there?"

Chapter Twelve

~ *Jenna* ~

I HAVE MY hands full.

Word about Tessa's arrest has not gotten out, and I am determined to protect her privacy. It's just a matter of time before the truth comes out and Tess is released. In the meantime, it won't help anyone for the town gossips to paint Tess as killer.

I know firsthand how that feels. When Riley Buxston was murdered and I was implicated for a nanosecond, the town gossips tried and convicted me in the court of public opinion, in some instances making up the facts when there were none to support their theories.

It's a horrible thing to live through, and I am determined not to let the gossip hounds add to her misery.

That means I'm doing double duty at the festival, taking care of my job, and filling in for Tess to handle the food vendors. And all on about three hours of sleep.

My mom is being a savior and taking over Tess's duties as soon as she closes up the shop at 6:00. I can't remember the last time I was so eager to see someone—well, maybe Ian, but for entirely different reasons, obviously.

I glance at the time on my phone. His plane should be touching down at the Asheville Regional Airport any minute. But no *I'm home* message yet, which has become our tradition when he returns from business trips. Even so, I know he will go straight to the police station where they are holding Tess.

As people began to arrive at the festival, we quickly realize in light of Allan's death and the ShakesPierre show rolling on without him our hunch that attendance would spike is playing out.

I'm grateful that Jack contacted the Brevard Police Department and got them to send officers over to help. Not that we fear the night will devolve into a mosh pit of out-of-control punks, but with a killer on the loose, it doesn't hurt to be careful.

Jack being so amenable also makes me believe that he isn't completely sold on the reality that Tess is a murderer. Otherwise, why would he spend a chunk of his budget on security?

Crowds are already gathering, laying blankets on the lawn in front of the stage, eating picnics they packed themselves or food they purchased from the vendors. Kelly Vega, one of the part-timers who helps Tess out at the Briar Patch, flags me down as I walk the perimeter.

"Have you seen Tess?" she asks.

"She had to step away," I say. "Is there something I can help you with?"

"I need more cookies. I'm all out. There should be some in the freezer. Can you go get them?"

She turns to pour coffee for the next party in line. When she returns with their cups, I ask, "Are you all alone?"

"Yeah, Eddie was supposed to be here at 4:00, but so far he's a no show."

"Wow, he's almost two hours late. Have you tried calling him?"

"Many times. He's not picking up, and his voicemail is full."

That's weird. Of course, in light of the circumstances, everything seems weird. But I do remember Tess saying that Eddie can be a handful sometimes. So much so that she has considered firing him. Hoping to encourage him to move along, she's already cut his hours to part-time. Could Eddie have killed Allan and framed Tess out of retribution?

But he doesn't know Allan, does he? It doesn't make sense that he'd do something so drastic just to get back at her. Yet he is a no-show tonight and isn't answering his phone. I make a mental note to mention it to Jack when I see him.

Kelly puts four cups of coffee in a cardboard carrier and says to the customer, "I'm sorry, but we're all out of cookies right now. I'm hoping to get more soon. Will you come back later? We should have some." She shoots me a pleading look.

"If you can't go, can you cover for me while I run to the bakery to get more cookies?"

Kelly is just a teenager. It's starting to get dark and I am not about to send her over there alone.

"I can go get them for you," I offer.

"You're the best, Jenna," she says. "Free cookies for you. Thank you so much."

Before I turn to go, I ask, "What's Eddie's last name?"

She frowns and rolls her eyes. "Davis. Eddie Davis. He is such a loser."

Then, in the next breath, she smiles and helps the next customer.

But even though I start off in the direction of the bakery, I don't really want to go in there by myself either. I text my mom and ask her to wait for me at her shop so we can go across the street together. I am not eager to put her in danger, but I figure there is strength in numbers. If we turn on all the lights and make enough noise, if someone is inside the shop maybe we can give them fair warning to leave through the door that opens onto the alley… the alley where Allan was murdered.

My mother's text buzzes and startles me enough to make me jump. *I'll wait for you in front of the bridal shop.*

I text a reply. *Be there in like two minutes.*

When I arrive, she is talking to Lily King, who owns Lily's Tearoom, which is next door to my mom's Blissful Beginnings Bridal Boutique, directly across Main Street from the Briar Patch bakery and Tess's apartment.

"I'm away for three days and we have another murder," Lily says. "Oh, hi, Jenna. Good to see you, hon. Terrible news about the murder, isn't it?"

I nod and silently hope Lily doesn't know that Jack arrested Tess. If she does, word will be all over town by way of Hemlock's Gossip Brigade.

"I'm so happy I had that surveillance camera installed before I left," Lily says. "I'm happy to give you the guy's card. I mean, one murder in town is a tragedy, two murders make it seem like a crime wave, but three? And this one is right across the street." She points with her nose at the alleyway. "What on earth is happening to our lovely little town? It used to be such a safe place."

As Lily chatters on, it dawns on me. The large bay window of her tearoom is directly across the street from the murder scene.

"Lily, does your surveillance camera record inside or outside your shop?" I ask.

"Oh, well, I'm not sure, honey. I got the top-of-the-line model. I figured I might as well. My insurance company offers an incentive for security equipment. And you know, I live upstairs over my shop just like Tess does, that poor dear. How is she? She must be traumatized to have that happen right next to her bakery. Just the other day, I was telling her she needs to get a camera. She said she couldn't afford one. Honestly, I don't see how you can go without. A single woman living alone just can't be too careful these days. To think it happened right across the street."

"Lily, perchance have you told Chief Bradley about your surveillance camera?" Mom asks. She has twigged to what I'm thinking.

"Oh, honey, no. I didn't have a chance. Two days after I had it installed, I left to visit my grandbaby in Florida."

"Lily, could we have a look at your security film? If it has a clear view to the alleyway across the street, it might show us who killed Allan Bossert."

As much as I want to go into Lily's office and get right to the footage, I have to get the cookies to take back to the Briar Patch booth. I promised Kelly.

I've already been gone longer than I'd planned.

Lily and my mom accompany me across the street to the bakery, saying there is no way they are letting me to go into the building by myself.

I have a sinking feeling this entire town will feel unsafe until the killer is behind bars.

While Lily and Mom wait in the dining room, where we've locked the door behind us and turned on all the lights, I dash into the empty kitchen and grab the cookies out of the freezer. I ignore the urge to look around. Not tonight. The kitchen that is usually so warm and full of good smells and the promise of everything sweet has a sinister feel tonight. I've helped Tess out in the kitchen before—or maybe a better way to say it is, I have sipped and nibbled while she measured and mixed—but tonight, rather than the warm, convivial hustle and bustle of baking for the morning rush, the florescent lights hum an ominous sound and emit a dingy green glow across the spotless kitchen.

As I pull the boxes of cookies out of the freezer, my phone buzzes. A text from Ian.

"Hi, beautiful. The plane just landed. As much as I wish I could come straight to you, I need to go to the police station first. Will text you when I'm through and will catch up with you at the festival."

I text back, *"So glad you're back. I've missed you."*

I consider telling him about the possibility the footage might hold, but it's a bit complicated to get into over text. Plus, if it ends up being nothing, there is no sense in getting Tess's hopes up only to dash them. Because Ian surely would share the news.

The thought of looking into his sea-glass green eyes and kissing his full lips warms and grounds me where the kitchen makes me feel cold and shaky. The fact that he is back is all the more reason to get out of this place that's giving me the creeps.

We make sure everything is locked up tight, double-checking the doors before we leave.

We stop in front of Lily's tearoom; I can hear convivial sounds of the festival in the distance. As I set off to deliver the cookies, I say to my mom and Lily, "I won't be too long. Just as long as it takes for me to drop these off and run back.

Will you please wait for me to look at the footage?"

"Of course," my mom says. "I can't blame you for wanting to see it firsthand."

She doesn't say it, but I know she is thinking that the images on this video could be the evidence we need to set Tess free.

"You go on," Lily says. "The guy who set up the video gave me a web address and a password, but I am going to have to figure out where I stashed them and then how to plug it all in. There's going to be a learning curve here because I am not technologically inclined like you young people. I'll probably need your help navigating the system."

"I can't say that I'm a techie," I say, "But I'll do what I can to help. I'll be right back."

The park is on the other side of the short block that houses the bridal salon and Lily's teashop. People are parking on Main Street and walking to the festival, and the lights and sounds emanating from the festivities make the short walk feel less spooky than it should be, given all that has happened.

When I finally reach the Briar Patch booth, I shift the cookie boxes in my arms and hold them out to Kelly, who takes them one by one. "There's three dozen in each pack. That gives you nine dozen. Is that enough?"

"For now," Kelly says. "Can I text you if I need more?"

"Sure," I say, although I am going to see if committee member Marcy Holden can cover for Mom and me while we look at the footage from Lily's camera.

Marcy, who had been in charge of last night's silent auction, is the one who had stirred up the drama, encouraging people to bid on the last-minute auction item of Tess's duet with Allan. She knows nothing about Tess's arrest, and of course, she isn't responsible for the predicament, but since she facilitated last night's drama, it's only fair that she helps me as I try to undo the damage.

Technically, Marcy has fulfilled her committee duties last night and is free to enjoy the festival, but since she is on the board of the Hemlock League Ladies Society, she knows there is an unspoken rule that all board members are on standby for crises just like this—because isn't it a given that everything always happens at once at the most inopportune time?

I set off toward the stage to look for Marcy. When I had announced that we'd secured the band for the festival, she went all fan-girl, proclaiming them a personal favorite. If I know her as well as I think I do, she will have staked out a prime front-row spot right for the concert, which is due to start in less than a half hour.

The sound tech is playing pop favorites over the sound system and some people are dancing to the music. Families are sitting on lawn chairs and blankets, eating fall treats, and sipping mulled cider, talking, and laughing—except for Lisa Davis, a teenage neighbor, who is lying in the grass making out with her boyfriend of the moment. A group of girls and guys who look to be about her age wander by the two and yell, "Get a room!"

Excitement hangs in the crisp, fall air, and if not for the tragedy of Allan's murder, Ian and I would be enjoying the night just like everyone else.

Marcy, where are you? The sooner I can see the surveillance footage, the sooner Tess will be free. I don't want her to spend the night in the Hemlock Police Department holding cell.

As I scan the crowd again, someone catches my eye.

Hanging out next to the side steps that lead up to the stage is a tall, skinny kid wearing a ShakesPierre T-shirt. He has spiky black hair and black-rimmed sunglasses—it's the kid who crossed the police line this afternoon.

I glance around to see if Jack is nearby.

He isn't. An officer from the Brevard Police Department is within earshot, but that won't work. Even if I explain the situation and show him the photo from this afternoon, what can he do? He'll probably call Jack, and by that time, we will have been staring at the kid so much, trying to act nonchalant that no doubt we will arouse his suspicion and he'll run.

Why not eliminate the middleman?

I dash off a text to Jack. *"The kid who breeched the police line is hanging out by the west side of the stage."*

Jack responded. *"I'll be right there. Don't approach him."*

Too late. I'm already standing next to him at the stage and doing my best ride-or-die ShakesPierre fan imitation.

"I can't believe the band is still going on tonight after

what happened," I say to him. "But I'm so glad they are. They're my favorite band, but this is the first time I've seen them. This is like a memorial to Pierre, don't you think?"

He pulls an earbud out of his ear and turns toward me, regarding me through his dark glasses. "I've seen them more than one hundred times."

"So, like what do you do?" I ask. "Do you work for the band or something?"

"Nah."

"What? You just follow them around?"

"Yeah. Basically. It's cool, ya know?"

"Personally, I can't believe Pierre is dead," I say.

The kid doesn't take the bait, so I turn on the urgency. "So, if you follow the band around, did you see his last concert?"

"Yep." He gives me a one-shoulder shrug like it is no big deal.

He certainly isn't much for conversation.

"What was the show like?" I ask. "I think it's going to be one of my big regrets in life that I never got to see Pierre perform. What do you think is going to happen to the band without him?"

"Don't know," he says. "I guess we'll see how they do tonight. Titania is singing. In some ways, she might be the better front person for the group. She's definitely hotter than Pierre."

How does he know Titania is singing? As far as I know,

the band didn't announce the news.

"Oh? Is she?" I ask. "I hadn't heard that. Where did you hear it?"

The kid stares at me—or at least I think he is. I can't see his eyes through his dark glasses.

Finally, he says, "I have a source."

I want to push it, but if I do, he might get irritated and ditch me.

"Cool," I say. "So, you're a Titania fan then?"

He smiles. "Yeah. One night in Buffalo, New York, I talked to her in a bar after a concert. She let me buy her drinks."

I want to ask him if he is even old enough to drink, but now that he is talking, I don't want him to clam up.

"Oh, wow, that is so cool. I've never met a famous person before." Hopefully, I have stars in my eyes. "I have zero chill when it comes to rock stars. I get so starstruck. Maybe it's a good thing I've never met one, because one of two things would happen. I'd either go totally shy and quiet, or I'd totally lose it and go berserk."

He gives me the side eye like I am a total nerd, which is exactly what I want. He won't be suspicious of or intimidated by a music nerd, and he might open up more.

I press on. "You must know Titania pretty well then if you drank with her. What's she like?"

His mouth quirks up at the corners. I really wish I could see his eyes.

ENDING ON A DIE NOTE

"She's pretty effing amazing." There is a dreamy tone to his voice. My nerd act is working, because for the first time since I've approached him, he seems to be letting down his guard.

"You sound like you're in love with her." I elbow him. "Are you? Huh? You gonna marry her?"

He laughs. "God, I'd marry her in a heartbeat if she'd have me."

"Not to kill your vibe," I say, "but I thought she and Pierre were involved."

"God, no. She can't stand him. Um—or I guess I should say she couldn't stand him."

Finally, we are getting somewhere.

"What, was there like rivalry between them?"

"All I'm saying is, the guy could be kind of a jerk."

"So, she must not be too sad that he's gone," I say.

He jerks back and frowns at me. "Have some respect. The guy is dead. Even if she hated him, she's not a monster. She's not like celebrating or anything."

"You're the one who called him a jerk."

The kid shrugs.

I lower my voice and lean in. "So, did Titania confide in you about the rivalry? I'm a huge fan, and I've never heard anything like this before. So, I'm dying to know."

The kid makes a face. "Their rivalry is pretty well known."

Clearly, he has pegged me for a poser.

"I know," I say. "I mean, that's so intimate. I'm intrigued. Do you know Titania well enough for her to tell you things like that?"

He bites his bottom lip and goes quiet again. I still wish I could see his eyes.

"So, you're not going to kiss and tell then?" I elbow him again, and he takes a few steps back, putting some space between us.

"It's not like that, man," he says. "Don't be so uncool."

Okay, so clearly, I need to dial it back a notch. I can't get a feel for whether he is a big talker or if he really is protecting Titania's privacy. If there is something going on between the two, she is a good ten years older than him. Even though her stage presence gives her the air of someone younger.

No doubt the kid is lovesick. Just how far he would go to win Titania's love? Would he commit murder?

"Hey, I'm sorry," I say. "Ugh. I'm just so sad today. I, for one, was always team Pierre. I just can't believe he's gone. I was so excited to see him tonight."

The guy doesn't say anything. I'm wondering if Jack is close by when my cell buzzes with a text. I angle my phone away from this fan.

It's from Jack. *"I told you not to talk to him."*

I reply, *"No harm. We're talking about the band. Interesting info. Give me a minute before you swoop in."*

Jack responds. *"You have one minute. Starting now."*

I lean in. "Did you hear how he died? I heard someone

shot him."

The kid shakes his head. "No, he wasn't shot. Someone stabbed him. Right through the heart." He pounds his chest with his fist.

And how do you know that?

"Ew. That's harsh. Do you know where it happened?"

"Look, I gotta go," he says, shoving his hands into his pockets as he walks away, but not before Jack and his officer, Reese Gibson, close in and apprehend him.

Chapter Thirteen
~ *Maddie* ~

L ILY ISN'T KIDDING about being no good with technology. By the time Jenna returns, we are no closer to accessing the footage than we were before she left, and she was gone a long time.

Turns out, she has a good reason. Jack has apprehended the kid we saw nosing around the crime scene this afternoon.

Jenna fills us in, careful to leave out the parts about Tess so not to clue in Lily, who is sitting there wide-eyed as Jenna shows her the photo she managed to snap of the guy.

"Where were you when you snapped that photo?" Lily asks.

Jenna and I exchange a quick glance.

"We were in Tess's apartment," I offer. It wouldn't take much for Lily to figure it out.

"Speaking of Tess," Lily says, "where is she tonight? Since this happened almost on the front stoop of her business, I would think she'd be in the big middle of trying to figure it all out, or at least selling her wares at the festival, but her shop has been closed all day."

"Tess couldn't open because of the investigation, and then she had an emergency come up," Jenna says.

"Oh, poor dear," Lily says. "I do hope everything is okay."

"It will be," I say.

"Well, good," Lily says. "Please let me know if I can help in any way."

"Giving us access to your security film is one of the biggest helps," I say and immediately regret it. Just as I feared, Lily cocks her head to the side and squints at us.

"How on earth will the security footage help Tess with her emergency?"

"Oh, what I meant is, by the time she returns, we will have given the police a big lead toward catching the killer, and she will be able to feel safe reopening the shop."

Lily nods, but I'm not sure she is completely buying it.

"So, this kid seems to be some kind of ShakesPierre super fan and is obviously lovesick over Titania," Jenna redirects the conversation. "My conversation with him left me wondering just how far he might go to win her love. He implied that there was no love lost between Titania and Allan. And from the way he spoke about her and her role in the band, Titania might have been plotting some kind of vocal coup long before this happened."

"What are you saying?" I ask. "Do you think Titania asked this kid to kill Allan?"

"I don't know," I say. "I get the feeling this kid was involved somehow, mainly because we saw him at the crime scene. You know what they say—a killer often returns to the scene of the crime. But I have no proof that Titania put him up to it. He knows his lady love longs to have the spotlight all to herself. What a better way to show his love than to eliminate the person who is standing between her and what she wants most?"

Both Lily and I stare at Jenna.

She shrugs. "Just a theory."

"You're getting pretty good at this," I say.

"At what?" she asks. "At digging around and coming up with plausible theories? But, if I do say so myself, this one tracks."

"Yes, it does," I say. "Lily's footage might prove your theory."

"You're right," Lily says. "But I am at my wit's end trying to figure out how to access it. I have to wonder what good a surveillance camera does if you can't get the footage. Obviously, I'm out of my depth here. Do you think that, since we are all stumped, one of you could call that handsome Captain Bradley and ask him to help us?"

"I have a feeling he's not very happy with me right now," Jenna says. "I texted Jack when I saw the kid, and he gave me an order not to approach. You would've been disappointed in me if I'd listened to him, right?"

I chuckle. "Jack should know by now that you know

how to handle yourself. Did you tell him everything the kid said to you?"

"I did. And I also supplied my theory about the kid and Titania. But if I call him with another lead that I've beat him to, I can't say he will be very receptive. I think this calls for someone with a bit more sway over Hemlock's handsome chief of police. Tag, you're it, Mom."

The butterflies in my stomach rise and fly in formation again. So many feelings battle inside me. What if, because Jenna talked to the kid in the park, he accuses me of meddling in his investigation again? Or worse yet, he thinks this is some sort of ridiculous ruse just to see him again?

But every single worry is absurd. Jenna and I are the ones who discovered the existence of Lily's footage. We just might be handing him a key piece of evidence. Then again, it all depends on what the video footage reveals. It very well could be just a still life of Lily's empty tearoom.

I hold my breath and dial his number before I get too much more in my head and psych myself out of making the call.

He answers on the first ring.

"Maddie?"

"Yes, Jack. I know you're having a busy night. So, I won't keep you, but I've discovered something I think might help your investigation."

I tell him how Lily has installed a video surveillance camera. "There's a chance it might have captured what happened in the alleyway last night."

"I'll be right there," he says.

I disconnect the phone and let out a breath I didn't realize I'd been holding.

I smile. "He didn't even sound irritated."

Chapter Fourteen

~ *Jenna* ~

JACK ARRIVES WITHIN five minutes, and within another fifteen minutes, he has helped Lily reset her password and retrieve the footage.

"You need to keep your log-in information someplace safe," Jack says. "If I were you, I wouldn't trust anyone else with it. Because whoever has this can access your account, just like we're doing. They can also delete footage." He points out the delete function. "In fact, to be safe, I'm going to forward myself a copy right now."

After he sends the footage to himself, it takes a few minutes to fast forward to the timeframe we are looking for—between midnight and 4:30 a.m., when he and his officers arrive. When we slow the film, at first, we see random people walking by. The film is grainy, but it gives a clear, wide-angle view that includes the front of the Briar Patch Bakery and the alleyway where Allan died.

Around 12:30 a.m., a guy dressed in black walks into the frame. He stops in front of the bakery and looks in the window, using the flashlight feature on his phone. It also illuminates his features.

"That looks like one of the Collins brothers, those guys who are opening the bakery—oh, excuse me, *la patisserie*—next door to Tess," I say. "Can you tell which one it is?"

"I don't know one from the other," Jack says. "In fact, I don't even know their first names."

"Josh and John Collins," I say and start to explain that they are twins, but the brother in the footage moves to the front door, lingers there for a moment, and then tears off the sign Tess had posted about the Briar Patch's hours during the fall festival and their booth in the park and rips it up.

"I can't believe he did that," I cry. "I'm glad we got it on video because Tess needs to know exactly what kind of scoundrels she's dealing with. It's bad enough that he's opening a similar business next door but ripping up her sign is horrible. Obviously, he has it out for her."

"That's terrible," Mom says. "What did the sign say?" she asks.

"She was alerting her customers that the cafe would be closed Sunday morning, and she asked them to come visit the Briar Patch booth at the festival tonight. I'll go over there and put up a replacement before I go back to the park."

After the Collins bro meanders out of frame, Jack fast forwards the footage. We see a few late-night walkers. Many are dressed up and look as though they may have attended the gala at the Hemlock Inn. The hotel is located at the other end of Main Street, but it is a walkable ten-minute stroll.

There is nothing that serves our purposes until just after 3:00 a.m.—3:01 to be exact—when Allan Bossert saunters into the frame. He appears to be coming from the direction of the gala. He disappears at the end of the alley that leads to the steps to Tess's apartment. Exactly as she's said in her statement.

After Allan disappears out of the frame, Jack lets the footage run at real time. By this early hour of the morning, the foot traffic on Main Street has become nonexistent, which isn't a surprise for Hemlock. Since most of the shops in the downtown area close at 6:00 in the evening, and only the restaurants are open for business, the town rolls up its sidewalks well before midnight.

About ten minutes after Allan heads down the alleyway, a figure dressed in what appears to be a coat large enough to obscure the person's body, a hat, and sunglasses—large, hipster frames that obscure the face—comes from the same direction Allan had come. The figure loiters in front of the bakery for a moment and then disappears into the inky shadows of the alleyway.

I grab Jack's arm. "Look! That's got to be him."

"Are you talking about someone specific?" Jack asks. "Or the killer in general?"

"I think it's the kid from the concert. The one you arrested for breaching the crime scene," I say. "Don't you think so? Look at the sunglasses."

"I don't know." Jack rewinds the footage until the person in question is back in the frame. He pauses it. "Those sunglasses are pretty common, and because of them and that hat, I can't see the person's face. Actually, that person doesn't look tall enough to be Byron Daily. That's the kid's name. Well, he's not exactly a kid—he's twenty years old. His height on the report is six-foot-four. "It's really hard to tell from the video, but if you look at this person compared to the height of the guy who looked into Tess's bakery window, this person is a lot shorter than six-four."

"But too tall to be Titania," I say. "Or Tess."

Jack makes a noncommittal sound and restarts the footage.

"Why would you think it could be Tess?" Lily asks.

I freeze. I have totally forgotten that Lily may've been listening in. So, I quickly change the subject. "Where is Byron?"

"We're holding Byron Daily on trespassing and breaching a crime scene charges," Jack says.

I want to hug him for so deftly changing the subject.

"I want to make sure he doesn't go anywhere. But when I get back to the station, I'll ask him where he was between the hours of 3:00 and 4:00 a.m. this morning. But this next part coming up might be a little rough to watch. You might want to step away."

Despite Jack's warning, I stay put.

Lily and Mom, however, excuse themselves to the kitchen to brew a pot of tea.

As Allan's lanky figure reenters camera range, Jack stops the footage again. "Are you sure you want to see this?"

I look away and a moment later, Jack makes an *ugh* sound. When I glance back, the perp walks out off camera as if he's just out for an early morning stroll. Allan is lying in a heap just inside the alleyway.

A few minutes later, when Mom and Lily bring the tea into the office, Jack says, "The perp left on foot in the opposite direction of which he came."

"Do you have any idea who it was?"

"It's hard to say," he says. "This isn't exactly high definition film."

We all sit in silence for a few moments. Jack blows on his tea as he fast forwards the footage until he reaches the part we have all been waiting for.

The timestamp on the video reads 4:16 a.m. Tess emerges out of the shadows of the alleyway. She stops and falls to her knees over Allan's collapsed body. Exactly as she said, she tries to revive him. It appears that's when she discovers his wounds, but not before she gets his blood all over her hands and the front of her sweater.

"She's a lot shorter than the person in the coat," I say. "This is proof that Tess is telling the truth."

Suddenly, I clamp my mouth shut and slant a wary glance at Lily.

"Proof that she's telling the truth about what?" Lily asks.

"About the circumstances surrounding Allan Bossert's murder," Mom says. "Poor Tess was the one who found him."

"Why do you need proof she was telling the truth?" Lily asks. "Why would you doubt her?"

"Sometimes you just have to work through every angle," Jack says. "I have seen all I need to see. Good work, you three. Now please stay out of my investigation."

Chapter Fifteen

~ Jenna ~

TESS IS RELEASED just before midnight. Since the video evidence creates a reasonable doubt, Jack sends her home with a firm warning that she is still considered a person of interest and needs to stay in town and make herself available for future questioning.

With that, an exhausted, tearful Tess is finally free.

After we run by the Briar Patch to post a sign letting customers know that the bakery will be closed on Sunday but will reopen on Monday—I make sure to tape it down with packing tape I've borrowed from Jack when we were at the police station, just in case the Collins brother happens to be wandering the streets in the wee hours of the morning; they'll have to work hard to get this sign off the glass door—Ian and I bring Tess to my apartment, where she promptly passes out, fully dressed, on the full-sized bed in the guest room.

When we are finally alone in the living room, I sit down next to Ian on the sofa.

"This isn't exactly the homecoming I'd planned for you."

He slides his arm around me. "Maybe I should think twice before I leave town without you in the future."

He plants a soft kiss on my lips. "It's not just because everything kind of fell apart, but because I missed you."

"Well, you know I can handle myself," I say. "But the missing you part is pretty hard to take."

"Yeah?" He leans in and kisses me again, deeper this time, pulling me closer so that my curves are pressed against the solid muscles of his chest.

Ian is the nephew of Valorie Anderson, Mom's best friend and my godmother. I think Val has been hatching a matchmaking plan since she first introduced Ian and me when I was in elementary school and he was starting middle school. He had been bookish and quiet and awkward. He didn't have much to say to me back then. But a while ago, when I was implicated in the murder of my ex-boyfriend, Riley Buxston, Val had contacted Ian, and he came to my rescue, working his magic much like he did tonight for Tess.

In addition to getting out of legal trouble, I got the added benefit of seeing the sparks of attraction between Ian and me ignite into a relationship. After all these years, it's clear that Ian McCoy is no longer that quiet, awkward, skinny boy with dark, curly hair and glasses. He's grown up nicely, tall with broad shoulders and chiseled cheekbones and a certain laidback vibe that always takes my breath away. Even with all that, our relationship got off to a couple of false starts. Why was I such a bonehead? Why did it take me a so long to finally give myself permission to be happy?

The good news is we are in love and looking toward the future together. Ian has committed to moving to Hemlock when his lease in Asheville is up, and he is even considering opening his own law practice. Now that he is back from the conference, he's going to look at a property just off Main Street in the downtown area.

A knock on the door at the top of the steps pulls us out of our romantic reunion.

"Jenna? Are you awake?" It's my mom's voice, and even though I am a grown woman of twenty-seven, I stand to put some distance between Ian and myself and quickly straighten my clothes and smooth my hair.

"Yes," I say. "Down here with Ian."

He sits back, casually throwing an arm across the back of the sofa, looking as if we had been discussing the theory of jurisprudence.

My cheeks burn. The two of us probably look like two teenagers caught making out in the basement—though we are far from our teenage years and my downstairs apartment is hardly my mother's basement.

It's 12:30 a.m. Thank goodness she doesn't make a habit of barging in on me like this. In fact, there's a very real possibility something else has happened.

"I'm so sorry to bother you." She directs the words to Ian more so than me. "And welcome home, Ian. But I need to tell you that I just picked up a message from Don Rhodes, the guy who covers this area for Uber. He says he was on duty Friday night into Saturday morning and didn't pick up any passengers in this area, which surprised him. He thought he'd get one or two because of the gala, but he said it was a quiet night."

"So, that means that Titania is lying about how she got back to the house," I say.

"Yes," Mom says. "She was lying about taking an Uber. I'm sorry. I guess the news could've waited until morning, but I thought Tess might still be awake. I mean, of course, she's exhausted. But I was wide awake after hearing the news, and even though I'm happy that Tess was released, and that kid was taken to the station, I'm more than a little creeped out by this. And clearly, I am rambling. I'll go back upstairs."

"No, it's okay, Mom. Come in. This new piece of the puzzle seems to confirm a few of our suspicions, doesn't it?"

"It sure does."

She stands there with her arms at her sides, clenching and unclenching her hands, a tell that she's completely freaked out. She's never been the kind of mother who barges in when I have company—male or female. For her to be here after Ian has been away this weekend, I know she is about to crawl out of her skin after hearing the news.

I hug her.

"Everything is going to be okay," I say. "Tess is all but cleared, and Jack is on this."

"You're right." She blinks and takes a step back, flexing her hands and giving them a quick shake, as if she's shaking off her heebie-jeebies.

She moves toward the stairs. "I should go and leave you two alone. I'm sure you have a lot to catch up on—"

"No, it's okay, really." Ian points toward the chair across from the sofa. "In fact, I think there's a few missing pieces you can fill in. I might need them if anything else stacks up against Tess. And at the very least, maybe I can offer a fresh perspective."

She sits, and we tell Ian what happened when we went out to the house where the band is staying. How Titania seemed to have made the decision for the band that the show would go on that evening with her taking over as solo vocals. Then I explain the weird coincidence of Byron Daily showing up at the crime scene and later learning that he has a thing for Titania.

"So, wait, the ShakesPierre band members are named Titania and Nick?"

We nod.

"I'm afraid to ask, but what are the names of the others?"

Mom looks at me, "Jenna has a much better memory than I do."

"Let's see," I say. "There's Nick Park, who plays guitar, and Demetrius Howe on drums—"

Ian groans and shakes his head. "So we have Titania, Nick, and Demetrius? Those are all characters from Shakespeare's *A Midsummer Night's Dream.*"

I have never been a Shakespeare fan, but it is pretty cool that Ian knows this.

After Mom goes back upstairs, Ian and I both realize how exhausted we are. He goes home, I go to bed, and, against all odds, sleep the sleep of the dead. Until I jolt awake at 6:30 the next morning remembering the news that my mother has broken about Titania's Uber lie. That and Byron Daily's Titania obsession ricochet in my brain. Titania isn't telling the truth, and I can't shake the feeling that there is more to Byron's story than he confided in me yesterday. Their lives certainly are more intertwined than I first realized.

I take a quick shower and dress.

The guest room door is still shut. So I decide to let Tess sleep until she wakes up. After all, she has the day off.

Suddenly, I pause. After things have turned upside down with the discovery of Lily's surveillance footage, Byron being arrested, and Tess being released, I've forgotten to check in with Kelly to see if Eddie had finally appeared.

Kelly had not texted me for help. Then again, she could have flagged down Marcy, who had graciously stepped in to cover for me, miraculously without asking for a detailed explanation.

Even though it's a stretch, I make a mental note to add Eddie to our list. He has a reputation of being flaky, but in light of everything that's happened, this flakiness calls for some checking into.

I take a chance and go upstairs to see if Mom is awake. Her shop is closed on Sundays. Even so, given the tidbit she learned last night, I worry that she hasn't slept at all.

"Hello?" I call softly. The heavenly scent of brewed coffee clues me in that she is indeed awake. Homie and Aggie scurry to greet me, each one jumping up on my legs, jockeying for attention. "Get down, you two. Where are your manners this morning?"

"Good morning," Mom calls. "We're in the kitchen. Want some coffee?"

We're in the kitchen?

"You read my mind," I say as I walk through the living room, round the dining room, and see Jack looking freshly showered, dressed in his uniform, sitting at the kitchen table with a coffee cup in one hand and a cinnamon roll in the other.

I am not going to ask, but is he an early visitor or... I glance at my watch—make that a very early visitor. Or did Mom call him last night to tell him about Titania's phantom Uber and he rushed over then? Maybe they've talked this morning and finally put the nonsense that has kept them apart behind them. I hope that means my mom is finally ready to move on with her life.

No disrespect to my dad's memory, but he's been gone for nine years. Mom deserves to live again, and before the navy chaplain showed up, Jack has been the only man who has been able to encourage that.

"Good morning, Jenna," he says.

I pause in case he feels the need to explain his early morning presence.

He doesn't.

"Good morning," I say, eyeing the pastry in his hand. "Where did you get the contraband? The Briar Patch is closed today."

"Four Seasons Patisserie, the one next door to the Briar Patch, opened today," he says.

Nice. First you arrest her. Then you defect to the competition.

"I'm scoping out the rival," he says. "Tess has nothing to worry about. This does not hold a candle to her cinnamon rolls."

He smacks his lips and looks up at the ceiling. "I'm no connoisseur," he says, "but something tastes off with these. Something tastes synthetic."

Yet it's not stopping you from stuffing your face, Chief Bradley.

I bite my lip to keep the words from slipping out. I'm a little cranky this morning. But my mom? She looks happier than I've seen her look in a long while. That is a great sign and it makes my heart feel lighter.

I go to the cupboard and grab a mug then pour myself a cup of coffee from the Chemex pour-over coffeemaker. I join them at the table, and Jack pushes the plate of cinnamon rolls in front of me. I push them back.

"No, thank you," I say. "I thought Four Seasons wasn't due to open until next week."

Jack shrugs. "Obviously, they had a change of plans."

"Was there a crowd?" I ask.

Jack grimaces and nods.

"So, after ripping up Tess's sign, the Co Bros. must've decided to take advantage of the Briar Patch being closed today. The weasels-of-all-seasons saw a chance to line their pockets and take advantage after Tess had been out raising money for the greater good. Nice."

"I guess that's capitalism," Jack says.

I cut a look at him and frown. "That doesn't excuse them. This is dirty pool. And not a very nice way to introduce themselves. Tess is beloved in the community."

"Well, Jack is right," Mom says. "These cinnamon rolls aren't very good. Taste them—just one bite."

I roll my eyes and pinch off a piece from one, pop it into my mouth, and chew.

"Ew. You're right. I mean, they're not poison, but they taste... processed."

I pick up the roll I have touched and study it. "And they're small. The ones Tess makes are twice this size."

All three of us take another bite—strictly for research, not for enjoyment. We frown.

"I know this taste," I say. "But I can't quite place it."

"I know what you mean," Mom says and puts her uneaten roll back on her napkin. "Frankly, it's not worth the calories."

"I know what it tastes like," Jack says as he wiped his hands on a napkin. "Remember those cinnamon rolls you can buy in the dairy aisle of the supermarket? The ones in the package like biscuits come in?"

My jaw drops. "Oh my gosh, you're right. These taste just like the bake-and-serve kind from the grocery store. How much are they charging for them?"

"Apparently, today only, to celebrate their surprise grand opening, they are giving away a free half-dozen to all who stop in."

"Which, pound for pound, would equal about two of the cinnamon rolls Tess sells," I say.

"What about the cinnamon rolls Tess sells?" Tess asks as she rounds the corner.

I have the sudden urge to grab the pastries off the table and toss them, plate, and all, into the garbage, but I am frozen in place. I'm sure the three of us look like we've been caught cheating. In a way, we have; we've two-timed the Briar Patch with Four Seasons.

"They were free," I blurt.

Mom and Jack nod.

"What was free?" Tess asks as she joins us the table and peers at the plate holding the evidence. She smiles. "Aww, did you make grocery store cinnamon rolls?"

The three of us don't say a word. We don't even move.

"It's okay if you did. Don't be embarrassed. I used to love those things as a kid. In fact, they're what inspired me to learn how to bake. I used to beg my mom to buy them, but we were so poor, we were always on a tight budget, and she said we didn't have the money for extras like that. But we always had flour, sugar, and cinnamon. So I figured I could learn to make them—"

"Tess, these aren't from the dairy aisle," I say, electing myself to break the bad news. "Or maybe they are, but that's not where we got them."

"Okay, where are they from then?" Her smile falters, making the dark circles under her eyes more noticeable. She looks as if she needs to sleep a hundred hours to fully heal from the trauma of the past twenty-four hours. I hate to give her more bad news.

"Let me get you some coffee," Mom says, getting up from the table. "I'll need to brew another pot anyway. I think we're going to need it."

"What's happened?" Tess demands.

"Don't worry, no one else was murdered. Not yet, anyway."

She looks horrified. "What does that mean?"

It's supposed to be a joke, but it falls flat. I regret saying it the moment I see her horrified expression.

"You know the Four Seasons Patisserie, the French bakery that's opening up next door to you?"

She scowls and nods. "I'll never forgive Bobby Orleans

for leasing to a competing business. What about them?"

"Well, I have good news and bad news," I say.

Warily, Tess lowers herself onto a kitchen chair. "Give me the bad news first."

"Unbeknownst to anyone but them, Four Seasons moved up their grand opening from the first of the month to this morning."

Tess's mouth falls open. I know exactly how she feels.

"I'm afraid to ask, but what's the good news?"

"The good news is these are their cinnamon rolls and they're terrible." I push the plate in front of her. She peers at its contents again, this time with more scrutiny. She pokes at one of the rolls with her finger and finally picks off a piece, tastes it, and makes a face.

"I don't understand," she says. "Is this a joke? Are you all trying to prank me?"

A knowing smile lifts the corners of her mouth. She's fully prepared to be a good sport.

"I wish we were," Jack says. "But when I drove by on my way over here, I saw a line out the door."

Okay then. Captain Bradley didn't spend the night here.

"I stopped to see what was going on," he continues. "These were free. They're giving away a half-dozen to everyone who stops in today."

"Yeah, once word gets around, I have a feeling they won't even be able to give them away," I say.

Tess looks bewildered. "But the sign in the window says

they aren't opening until the first of the month."

Then she sets her mouth. Yep, she's just figured out the score. "So, they saw that the Briar Patch is closed today, and they decided to jump on it… with these." She makes another face and pokes at the roll on the plate again.

"I mean, I guess there's nothing wrong with store-bought bake-and-serve rolls… if you're five years old or feeling nostalgic. But to try to pass them off as your own? That's just wrong."

"Well, I'm sure it won't win them any business," Mom says as she sets a steaming cup of coffee in front of Tess. "They might be a novelty for a week or so because people are curious, but when they compare the Briar Patch's offerings to this"—Mom nods at the plate where the frosting on the rolls has hardened and taken on a shiny look, while the cold rolls have appeared to shrivel—"there's no contest. Not for people who have tastebuds."

"You all are the best," Tess says. "I appreciate you trying to make me feel better, but it's the principle of the matter. I knew I should have opened the bakery today. This is two days in a row we've been closed. And Sunday is my busiest day."

She sighs and looks as defeated and exhausted as she did yesterday.

"I know we have a lot of things to discuss," Mom says. "Tess hasn't even heard the latest development. Actually, that's why I invited Jack here this morning. But first things first. Have we considered that the Collins brothers might have a motive for setting Tess up?"

Tess's eyes widen.

"That's pretty cutthroat," Jack says.

"She has a point," I say in my mother's defense. "Think about it. Tess has built a healthy clientele over the years she has been running the Briar Patch. Given the way they have been scoping her out and how they seemed to come out of nowhere with this surprise grand opening, wouldn't that take planning? Even if they are only serving store-bought cinnamon rolls. They would've had to have the goods on hand."

"A product like that can be frozen," Tess says. "I don't like the fact that they have clearly come to town to compete, but I'm not convinced that's a motive for murder."

"Imagine how much easier their lives would be if their main competitor, and the only other bakery in Hemlock, North Carolina, suddenly went out of business because the proprietor was in jail," Mom says. "I think, at the very least, we should look into it. Let's find out if they have an alibi for early yesterday morning. In Lily's video footage, we saw somebody looking in the window of the Briar Patch before Allan was killed. Jack, have you talked to either of the Collins brothers?"

"I spoke to both Josh and John individually when I stopped in this morning," he says. "Not only do both have alibies with John's wife, Sally, but all three of them can back it up with time-stamped credit card receipts from the all-night diner the four of them went to over in Rutherford after the gala. Since we've had such good luck with security footage, I've sent one of my men over to the diner to take a look at theirs.

"But I guess a lot of what I do next depends on your new discovery."

Chapter Sixteen
~ Maddie ~

I FILL IN Jack on what we learned when we went out to the house where the band is staying: "Not every member of the ShakesPierre band was as eager as Titania was to go on stage last night," I say. "She said that she and Allan stayed to have a drink at the bar in the Hemlock Inn rather than going back to the house with Angel and the others.

"But I finally got ahold of the Uber driver who works this area. He said he didn't pick up a single fare Friday night going into Saturday morning."

"You're sure he's the only one who drives around here?" Jack asks.

"As far as I know."

"Titania was a little hostile when Jenna and I talked to her," I say. "Rather than push it, I asked Angel if she would ask Titania for the Uber receipt."

"And?" Jack asks.

"Well, it's been a little crazy these last eighteen hours," I say. "I haven't seen Angel to ask her. I was going to follow up with her today."

"No, stay away from that house," he says. "I'll have my men follow up."

He must sense that ordering me around doesn't sit well with me, because he immediately changes his tune and the subject.

"I have to go." He scoots back his chair and stands. "I have a lot of things to take care of today. The band is chomping at the bit to get out of here. Their manager says they have another gig in Asheville, but I haven't cleared them yet, and with this new piece you've given me, it might be a while before I can. But would you like to get some dinner tonight?"

"IT'S A FREE country," Jenna says. "He can't make you stay away from that house. But if you don't want to go with me to talk to Titania, I'm fine going by myself."

"No," I say. "You are not going out there by yourself."

"Good, because I really don't want to be out there alone."

Spurred on by the air of competition and discovering that one of the Co Bros. ripped her sign off the door, Tess decides to open the Briar Patch. It will be after 9:00 by the time she gets there, and she still has to bake, but she's called Kelly and Eddie, who are both available to come in. Eddie has confessed that he needs the money since he missed most of his shift at the festival last night. He had a flat tire driving in from Landrum, which is the next town over. And as bad luck will have it, his cell phone had been dead, too.

Eddie tends to live under a swirling black cloud of bad luck.

If there is a silver lining about Tess's Co Bro. irritation, it's that the situation is forcing her to get back into the bakery. Going in there for the first time after Allan's death will be the hardest part. It will be like confronting Allan's ghost.

If only she could talk to him. He could tell us who murdered him.

Jenna and I drive Tess to the bakery. Even though she doesn't ask us to go inside with her, we do, so she doesn't have to walk into the kitchen alone.

I am happy that Tess seems totally unfazed. She unlocks the doors and begins pulling out sacks of flour and sugar and trays of spices as if it is just another day.

"What are you baking?" I ask.

She smiles. "Cinnamon rolls, of course. I have a feeling that once my customers taste what the Co Bros. are selling, they'll come home to mama."

"I think you're right," Jenna says. "And I have a feeling their impromptu grand opening might have backfired on them."

Kelly arrives, and Jenna and I leave them to do their

thing.

Even though it sounds as if the illustrious Collins brothers have an alibi for the timeframe Allan was killed, we decide to pop into Four Seasons Patisserie and ask the guys a few questions.

Because they are new to town and haven't tried to meet their business neighbors—other than Tess—they have no idea who we are. We figure we can act like customers and use our anonymity to our advantage.

The line Jack said had snaked out the door early this morning is gone. The only other customer in the shop is leaving as we enter.

"We're closed," says one of the brothers without looking up from the cash register. We step closer, and I can see his nametag says Josh.

The place is tiny. Other than the cash register, which is on a small cabinet, there is a display case to house the pastries—it's mostly empty now—a self-serve drink cooler, and a lot of Eiffel Tower paraphernalia. No place to sit and eat or drink coffee like at the Briar Patch. This operation looks strictly cash and carry.

On that note, I have no idea if they even take credit cards.

"Oh, but I heard you were giving away free cinnamon rolls," Jenna says. "Please tell me you have some left."

Looking annoyed, the guy glances up and does a double take. His hard demeanor softens, and he even manages to smile at my daughter.

"We gave away all the free rolls about an hour ago," he says. "Sorry. But I do hope you'll come back tomorrow. We won't have anything free, but we'll be restocked."

"What a shame," I say. "That was going to be our breakfast, and with the Briar Patch not being open today, I guess we're out of luck. But I guess it was good business for you since you moved your grand opening up to today."

Josh laughs. "Yep, their loss is our gain."

"What made you move it up?" Jenna asks.

He shrugs. "We were ready. Why not?"

"I guess I'm a little surprised that you opened this weekend after that murder happened right out there. Did you hear about it?" I feign a shudder and rub my arms.

Jenna murmurs her apprehension, too.

"Well, you know, people still have to eat. Or at least those who are still alive do." He chuckles.

I get the feeling that he thinks he's pretty clever.

"I just have to ask this because I've been wondering," I say. "What made you open a bakery next door to another bakery that is pretty beloved in this community?"

Josh smirks again. "The Briar Patch?"

We both nod.

"We don't consider that place competition. We are a French patisserie. That place is basically a donut shop."

I bristle, and it takes everything I have not to tell him that his store-bought cinnamon biscuits aren't even in the same league as Tess's bakes, but again, I play along.

"Oh, so you're looking to bring some French culture to Hemlock?"

Josh lifts his chin. "We're going to try."

"Since you're closed, can we take a peek at your kitchen?" I say "I don't suppose you have one of those La Cornue ranges, do you? I've only seen photos of them, but it's my dream to own one someday. If you have one, I'd love to see it."

"Indeed, we do," he sings. "Only La Cornue ranges for my kitchen. Come on back."

I try not to smirk. While La Cornue is the crown jewel of luxury ranges and sometimes costs as much as a small house, I can't imagine the brothers running a successful commercial bakery with one. And my hunch seems to be true when we walk into the kitchen and see one of the smaller ranges with one oven and five gas burners. Granted, it is a thing of beauty, but the small range coupled with the Poppin' Fresh rolls they served today, it is clear that the Co Bros.'s French is more show than substance.

Time will tell.

As Josh Collins extols the virtues of his work-of-art range and flirts shamelessly with my daughter, I take a moment to browse around the kitchen, looking for one piece of evidence in particular.

I find it almost instantly. Next to the back door sits an army of white garbage bags stuffed to capacity. Through the not quite opaque plastic I can make out dozens of wrappers from cans of cinnamon roll dough sold in the dairy section of the grocery store.

I hold my phone down and snap a photo. Josh must've caught me, because he says, "Look, ladies, I'd love to chat, but I have an appointment in a bit, and I have to close up the shop." He motions for us to follow as he walks toward the door that leads to the bakery. "I do hope you'll stop in again."

He speaks to my daughter, looking her directly in the eyes, and I can't decide if it is flirty or creepy. Probably a little of both.

When we are in the car, I say, "I found the evidence we were looking for."

I show Jenna the photo.

"Ten bucks says they cleaned out the local Ingles of all their bake-and-serve cinnamon rolls and then they stayed up all night baking them to give away."

"That's so odd," Jenna says. "Is this really going to be their gig? If so, they're not going to win many customers. Cinnamon rolls aren't even French, are they?"

"Maybe the store-bought rolls were just to facilitate a spur-of-the-moment decision to open early," I say. "Maybe they won't make the regular menu."

"Either way, I hate to tell them, but they just scared away all their potential customers. I'm relieved that Tess doesn't have anything to worry about. Because clearly Four Seasons

Patisserie"—Jenna says the competing bakery's name in a horrendous French accent—"it is, how do you say, *tres poo-poo*."

We laugh.

"They may have an alibi that clears them of Allan's murder," I say, "But if they stayed up all night baking so they could take advantage of Tess closing the Briar Patch, do you think we could have Jack arrest them for attempted murder of their competitor's business?"

Jenna laughs. "Yes, I have a feeling that's the only murder they're capable of. I think Josh Collins is too prissy to sully his hands or his bespoke French cuffs. I think we can cross them off the suspect list."

"Okay, but he sure seems to like you," I tease. "If things with Ian don't work out, you have a fallback. You could be *ze* Marie Antoinette *de* Hemlock. Let *zem* eat *ze* store-bought cinnamon rolls."

Jenna laughs at my horrendous French accent and waves off the thought. "No thank you. He is so not my type. Plus, is he the married one?"

"No, I think John Collins is married.

Jenna shudders. "Even if he's single. No thank you."

A companionable quiet settles between us.

"So, it was a surprise to see the chief in your kitchen this morning. Does that mean he still has a chance?"

"We'll see." I stare straight ahead, my eyes on the road.

"That's certainly not a no."

I slant a quick glance in her direction and see her knowing smile.

While we are downtown, we decide to stop by the bar at the Hemlock Inn and see which of the bartenders were on duty Friday night.

The bar opens at 11:00 a.m., but the staff comes in early to restock and get ready for the day. It would be a good time to catch the staff before customers begin to trickle in.

We find a parking space on the street in front of the hotel and enter through the revolving doors at the main entrance. The lobby is empty except for a couple rolling their bags across the marble floors toward the exit.

The bar is located through the arched doorway on the right. When Jenna and I enter, it appears to be as empty as the lobby. Two people are behind the bar—a woman, who appears to be counting bottles and writing notes on a clipboard, and a guy, who is polishing glasses with a white cloth before putting them on a shelf under the liquor.

"Excuse me," Jenna says. "My name is Jenna Bell. I'm the chair of the Hemlock League Ladies Society Harvest Moon Gala that was held in the hotel ballroom on Friday."

Both stop what they're doing.

"Hi, I'm Natasha Merrell, the bar manager. How can I help?"

"Were either of you working the bar the night of the gala?" I asked.

"We both were," Natasha says.

Jenna holds up her phone to show photos of Allan and Titania that she pulled from their social media pages. "Do recognize either of these people?"

They both lean in for a look.

The guy shakes his head.

"Oh, yeah," says Natasha. "That's the guy from that band who was murdered, right?"

"Unfortunately, yes," I say. "Was he in here late Friday night, early Saturday morning?"

"He was," Natasha says. "He got really drunk."

Her coworker resumes polishing the glasses, but he is listening as Natasha talks.

"What about the woman in the picture?" Jenna asks. "Was she with him?"

Natasha shakes her head. "He was alone."

"Are you sure?" I ask.

"Absolutely. I remember because there was a bit of a commotion when he first came in the bar, a little before midnight. Some fans of the band recognized him and asked for autographs. He signed one, but then he told them he wanted to be left alone. Seemed like he was not in the mood. So, he sat right there and drank bourbon." She pointed to a seat at the end of the bar. "A lot of bourbon."

"So he was here for a while?" Jenna asks.

"Yes, I had to cut him off because he was so sloppy, but it was 2:00 a.m., which is closing time anyway. But he sat there nursing his last drink until we finally had to ask him to leave because we had to lock up. That was after 2:45."

"Do you know if he called a car or if anyone came to pick him up?"

"I offered to call him an Uber, but he refused. He said he was going to walk."

Natasha stops and squints at us. "I've already told all of this to the police. Do you mind if I ask what you're going to do with all this info?"

"It's for our committee report," Jenna says. "He was supposed to play the concert in the park last night. You know, just looking out for the Hemlock League Ladies Society. Such a tragedy, isn't it?"

I breathed an inward sigh of relief for Jenna's quick thinking. I should've been prepared for that question, but I wasn't.

"But the blonde in the photo?" I asked. "She didn't come into the bar?"

Natasha shook her head.

"Um, I'm pretty sure I saw her," said the guy polishing the glasses. "She met a guy in here. He'd been sitting at the bar. He wanted a beer, but I wouldn't serve him because he didn't have an ID. He ordered a club soda instead."

"Tall? Dark hair?" I asked.

The bartender squints his eyes as if trying to recall. "Yeah. That sounds like him."

"Was he wearing black-rimmed sunglasses?" Jenna pulls up the photo she shot of Byron out the window of Tess's apartment and zooms in so that the crime scene tape is out of frame. She holds up the phone for him to see.

"Yeah, that looks like him. He wasn't wearing the glasses in here, but they were hanging from the neck of his t-shirt," he said.

"And the blonde?" Jenna thumbs back to the screenshot of Titania and holds up her phone again. "Did you serve her?"

"No," he said. "She came in and then she and the guy left together."

Chapter Seventeen

~ Jenna ~

After uncovering the treasure trove of information about Titania meeting Byron in the bar, we decide to drive out to the house where the band is staying to see if Titania will talk about where she and Byron went after they left the bar.

The bartender said they left around 12:15-ish. So, if Angel heard someone come in at 4:00, it had to be Titania. Where were she and Byron for three hours and forty-five minutes?

While Byron's presence solves the mystery of the phantom driver, it brings up more questions than were answered.

When we arrive, the house is surrounded by police cars. It appears that every cop on the Hemlock police force is here.

"Oh, no, what's happened?" I ask.

"I don't know," my mom says. "I hope everyone is okay. Let's go in and see."

I put my hand on her arm as she unbuckles her seat belt. "Are you sure? Jack asked us to stay away. It seems like the two of you are just starting to work things out. I don't want him to get mad."

My mother snorts. Yes, she actually snorts. "If things are going to work out between Jack and me, he is going to have to accept the fact that I do not take orders from anyone. Do you see any crime scene tape around here?"

I shake my head.

"Then that's a good indication that this is not a hostage situation and no one else is dead," she says as she lets go of the seat belt. It slides into its place against the car's interior with a *thwack.*

"Well, something's happened. Unless the Hemlock police force is throwing a goodbye party for the band and we weren't invited."

We let ourselves out of the car and walk up to the porch where Nick and the band's drummer, Demetrius, are sitting in the wicker chairs. They don't look upset, which was another good sign that no one else had died.

"Hey, guys," I say as we approach them. "What's with all the cop cars?"

The guys exchange a look.

"Titania is, like, missing," Demetrius says. "The cops came out to talk to us to see what we know. We thought she was sleeping in, but when Angel went into her room to wake her up, she wasn't there. She was, like, gone."

It is our turn to exchange alarmed glances. Then Mom says, "Do you have any idea where she went?"

"No clue," Demetrius says. "She probably just bounced. You know, tired of being here, tired of being hassled by the cops. Because they said we can't leave yet. I actually thought about getting out of here myself, but they said she is in trouble for leaving. What is this? Like high school detention?"

The guy beats a cadence on the arms of the chair, but he looks more vacant than inconvenienced. It must be hard to live with a drummer; pounding out rhythms is probably in his DNA.

"Do you think she's okay?" my mom asks. "I mean, the authorities still haven't caught Allan's killer."

"Who is Allan?" Demetrius asks.

"Allan Bossert?" I supply. "That's the real name of your late lead singer, Pierre Von Strussen."

"Oh, yeah, right." He clucks his tongue and pounds out another cadence on the arms of the chair.

That drumming is starting to get on my nerves.

"Can you not, please?" I say.

Clearly, the guy isn't too bright. Or maybe he is on drugs. Or possibly both.

Nick reaches out and puts his hand on Demetrius's, stilling it. "Dude, please."

Demetrius stops. "No problemo. Any-hoo, I'm starving. I'm going inside to see what's for food. There's no law keeping us from, like, noshing, is there?"

He laughs at himself. It takes a moment for Demetrius's

frenetic energy to dissipate after the screen door slams behind him like a cymbal crash.

Nick closes his eyes for a long blink, as if trying to regain his bearings. His eyes are red rimmed, but this time he seems to be keeping a stiff upper lip.

"How are you doing, Nick?" I ask.

He shrugs and shakes his head.

"Hey, it's going to be okay," I say to him.

He slants a look at me. "Is it? How do you know? She left all of her stuff behind. Even her iPad and her cash. Maybe someone took her."

My mom and I exchange an urgent glance.

"Nick, I'm sure Titania will be okay.

I say it to comfort him. Really, I have no idea if she is okay or not.

"Did she take her cell phone?"

Nick shrugs. "Don't know. I didn't get a chance to look around her room much before the cops arrived and kicked me out."

"Did you try texting her?" I ask.

"I did, but she didn't answer."

If she did leave her cell phone behind, it's probably so that no one can track her. Same with the credit cards. She can't use them if she's trying to disappear. Then again, there is always the possibility that someone took her away in the middle of the night.

"What did she do after the concert last night?" Mom

asks.

"She was kind of quiet," Nick says. "I sat next to her in the van that brought us back to the house."

"She did come home, then," I say. "She didn't go out like she did after the gala?"

"She said she was tired and was going to bed." Again, he shrugs. He looks so sad. It is easy to see that Nick is a sensitive soul who is taking everything hard. But I have to worry that maybe there was more to his ennui, such as unspoken feelings for Titania.

I hadn't thought about it until now, but yesterday Titania did seem to have a power over him. He'd been reticent about going on stage, but she had effectively changed his mind right here in front of us. Or maybe not changed his mind as much as she mellowed him out. Mollified him to the idea.

"I'm going to go inside and find Angel," my mom says. "Maybe I can get in and see Titania's room."

She doesn't say it, but I know she wants to see if there is any sign of a struggle.

"I'll be in in a moment." I sit down in the chair next to Nick, where Demetrius had been a moment ago.

"Can I ask you a personal question, Nick?"

He nods. "Sure."

"Are you in love with Titania?"

He stares straight ahead, then glances down at his red high top sneakers. "Titania and me… it's… complicated.

We've had an on and off *thing*. You know?"

No, I didn't know.

"What do you mean?"

"It's hard to have a relationship when you spend so much time on the road," Nick says. "If you're with someone who's not in the band, there's not enough time together, or there's too much togetherness if you're with someone in the band. Sometimes we… hook up."

His pale cheeks flame.

"I'm sensing that you would rather your relationship with Titania not be a friends-with-benefits situation? You want something more permanent… am I right?"

He kicks at the porch floorboard with the toe of his sneaker. "I've always held out hope that someday she'll come around and feel the same for me that I feel for her."

"You're in love with Titania, Nick. There's no reason to be embarrassed or ashamed. Love is a beautiful thing."

But what if she doesn't return his feelings? Is Nick the quiet, brooding type who will kill over unrequited love—hence Titania going missing? Or would he kill someone else who stands between him and love?

"Not to be insensitive, but were Titania and Allan ever romantically involved?"

His head snaps up and his lip curls. "No way. She couldn't stand him."

He clamps his lips between his teeth and looks around to see if anyone else heard him. But he and I are the only ones on the porch.

"To be honest, none of us liked Allan. He was so obnoxious. Always had to have things his way."

I have no poker face. Clearly, he's read the million-dollar question I want to ask.

"No, I did not kill Allan Bossert." He leans forward in his chair and looks crushed. His tone is just short of hostile, but it softens when he says, "And while we're at it, I had nothing to do with Titania's disappearance either. I would never hurt her."

I want to believe him. I really do. Actually, I am more concerned about what he would do to someone else who hurt Titania, physically or emotionally. Like Allan or—

"Do you know a guy named Byron Dailey?" I ask.

Nick rolls his eyes. His shoulders hunch. "Of course I do. Everyone in the band knows Byron Dailey because he's always around. He's a rich-kid groupie. He follows us from gig to gig."

"What is his relationship to Titania?"

Nick sits back hard in the chair and a huff of a breath escaped. "The guy is a child."

"Technically, he's not. He's twenty years old. What can you tell me about him and Titania?"

Nick's eyes narrow. "He is her current squeeze right now. At first, the guy was a running joke among the band. You know, the super fan who would hang out at the front of the stage, trying to get Titania's attention. But, God, she's like ten years older than he is. She didn't want anything to do with him... at first. Then he started sending her presents. Expensive gifts like jewelry and crazy flower arrangements. That got her attention. Titania loves *stuff*. So, for about the last six months, they've been hooking up after shows. He doesn't seem to have a job since he's always showing up where she is. I have no idea how he affords his lifestyle. Obviously, you know he's in town now."

"I do. I talked to him last night before the concert."

For now, I decide to keep quiet about Jack bringing Byron in for crossing the police line, because I don't want to further prejudice Nick's already poisoned opinion of Byron. Plus, I want to see exactly how much Nick knows—if, somehow, he's aware that Byron has been arrested.

"Do you have any reason to believe Byron would kill Allan?"

Nick's face opens. Maybe he hadn't thought of the possibility before now.

"The kid's a piece of work. It's obvious he's used to getting what he wants. Maybe—if he thought he could get in good with Titania by getting rid of Allan so she could have the entire spotlight? I could see it."

"Would he hurt Titania if she rejected him?"

Nick lets out a low whistle. "T can take care of herself, but that kid is a loose cannon. I don't know, man."

"I know this hasn't been easy for you, Nick, but I appreciate you answering my questions," I say. "If you need to talk to someone, I'm here for you. And if you can think of anything else, please call me."

I reach into my purse to get a business card, and when I look up, his face is contorted.

"What is it, Nick?" I put my hand over his. I am sure he is about to tell me something, but before he can, Jack bounds out of the house.

"I asked you two to stay away so that my team can do its job?" Jack isn't yelling, but his voice carries, and the low tone sounds scarier than if he bellowed full force.

My mother is right behind him, with Angel trailing behind her. Madeleine Bell does not look happy. On the rare occasion I would get in trouble when I was a kid, I always knew how deep I was in for it based on the look on her face.

Right now, if I were Jack, I would run.

It's a good thing he is a cop. That's probably the only thing that makes my mother take a deep breath. I am sure she is silently counting to ten before she says, "Jack, I have as much right to be here as you do. I need to talk to Angel about a couple of things that are important and have nothing to do with you."

That isn't exactly true, but it isn't exactly a lie either. Jack is a great guy, but he still hasn't learned how to get out of his own way. My mother has proven time and again that she has a knack for solving crimes. Sometimes she can see things Jack can't because he is too close to the situation. Since we aren't cops, we can get people to talk where they might clam up when the authorities burst in. Like the way Nick just talked to me, and how, it seems, he was about to tell me something important.

And once my mom figures out an angle to her satisfaction, she always turns it over to Jack to make the arrest and put away the criminal.

Maybe he is being a little more hard-nosed this time because things have been so tenuous between them... even though it doesn't seem that way this morning. Seeing them together around the breakfast table, it appeared that they were on their way to better days.

"Then you need to stay out here and stay out of my way," he says. "We have a person of interest who has gone missing, and we need to find her."

Dude, lighten up before you blow your chances.

I just wish he could see that he and my mom are better together than they are apart. They make a great team. I hope things like this don't keep them from the happiness they both deserve.

"Jack, did you make any headway with Byron Daily?" I ask to diffuse the situation, overturning my initial decision to stay mum about Byron. "Did he give you any information about the nature of his relationship with Titania?"

Jack looks grim, like the weight of the world is crushing him but he is trying to be stoic and strong.

"I released Byron Daily this morning. He lawyered up in a hurry. Apparently, his family is loaded. Since we were holding him on a third-degree misdemeanor and the guy has no previous record, his lawyer made a very convincing case that he should be released on his own recognizance. We had no reason to hold him."

Rabid Titania-fan Byron Daily is released into the wild right before Titania goes missing?

Nick's head jerks to me. His eyes are urgent.

"Jack, do you think Byron killed Allan, maybe out of jealousy or out of a perverse sense of loyalty to Titania, and now he's kidnapped her?"

All Jack says before he turns to leave is, "We're on it."

"Actually," Angel says after Jack disappears back inside the house, "maybe it would be best if you both come back later. It's so chaotic right now. It's not a very good time to talk. I have your phone number, Maddie. I'll give you a call later on after things settle down."

My mother nods. It's one thing for Jack to tell my mother to leave, but it is another thing when someone like Angel asks politely.

As my mom and Angel stand talking quietly about something I can't hear, Nick touches my arm. "Can you come back later?"

"Yes," I say. "Why?"

His gaze darts around the porch. Then he leans in and lowers his voice. "Titania is in trouble. I know where she went. If I tell you, you have to keep it on the down low because—"

Nick stops talking when Angel and my mother walk toward us. His eyes are huge.

"Hey, Nick, why don't to get something to eat?" I ask. "We could bring something back for everyone."

"The cops told us to stay put." Angel puts her hand on Nick's shoulder. "We have plenty of food here. The sooner we answer all their questions, the sooner we can get on the road. We have another gig to get to. Oh, and, Nick, the police want to talk to you next. Why don't you go inside and see if they're ready for you?"

"Sure," he says to Angel. "Hey, it was great to see you, Jenna. Don't be a stranger."

He leans in and hugs me, and whispers, "She's in Johnson City, Tennessee. Her family has some cabins they rent out. We went there once."

"Do you know the address or what they're called?"

"Nick?" Angel steps closer. "Please don't keep the police waiting. The quicker we talk to them, the quicker we can get out of here."

Chapter Eighteen

~ *Maddie* ~

A LITTLE INTERNET sleuthing turns up that Titania's real name is Dede Clift. Jack probably knows that, but he hasn't shared it with us.

Johnson City is about two hours north of Hemlock, an easy drive straight up Interstate 26. We decided to drive up and see what we can find out. Despite the unfortunate circumstances, it is a nice trip. The Appalachian Mountains are decked out in their fall finest, boasting the reds, oranges, and golds of autumn, and the roads are good. It has been a long time since I've been up this way, which proves that I've been working at the shop and writing way too much.

As Jenna drives, she elaborates on her conversation with Nick and his unrequited love for Titania.

"Seems like Ms. Clift is quite the hot item, with both Nick and Byron vying for her attention." A chill ripples through me, and it isn't caused by the fall air. It hits me that we are going to a rather rural area based on a tip from a guy we don't really know. If we find the cabins in question, who knows what or who might be waiting for us.

"Are you sure that Nick is as innocent as you think he is?" I ask.

"It's not like he sent us to a specific address," she says. "I'm pretty sure there aren't rock-star killers and kidnappers behind every door in Johnson City."

"You're right," I say. "We still need to find out where these mysterious cabins are located. Who knows if Titania will even be there?"

I use the drive time to search for more information about Dede Clift, Johnson City. When that doesn't turn up anything, I do similar searches in Johnson City for the name Clift, cabins, Tatiana, and ShakesPierre. Each inquiry turns out to be a dead end.

Next, I make a list of cabins for rent in the Johnson City area. Not including those offered by VRBO and Airbnb, there are twenty separate listings ranging from as far south as Erwin, Tennessee, and Gate City, Virginia, on the northern end. But in Johnson City there are only four specific listings.

"This is going to be interesting," I say. "It seems Johnson City might be just spread out enough to make the scant information we have tantamount to searching for a needle in a haystack. We might have to ask around."

"I wish I'd had time to ask Nick for more information," Jenna says as she steers the car into a public parking lot that serves the downtown area off of State of Franklin Road. "Don't you think it is weird that he doesn't want Angel to know that he might know where Titania is?"

Jenna maneuvers into a parking place and kills the engine.

"I think everyone is a little on edge right now."

"Since Tess knew Angel from back in the day, I called Tess before we got on the road and used her as a sounding board," Jenna says. "She says Angel has always been the glue that's held that band together. She's kind of like a mother hen, making sure all of her little chicks are okay." Jenna gives her head a quick shake.

"What's wrong?" I ask.

"I don't know. There are so many loose ends. We're not sure if Titania ran or has been kidnapped. If she ran, why? Are she and Byron together? Did he kill Allan? Did Titania put him up to it? We still don't know what they were doing between the time that they left the bar at the Hemlock Inn and when Angel heard her come in… which seems to be after Allan was killed." She covers her face with her hands and groans. "There are so many loose threads. And all of them seem to involve Titania and Byron."

"Since we're here, why don't we ask around? Maybe someone local knows the Clift family and where the cabins are located. It would beat knocking on random cabin doors."

Downtown Johnson City seems to be caught somewhere between quaint Southern town and artsy hipster cool. There's a state university a few miles down the road, which probably is the reason the small-town patina appears to be in the process of polishing up to cater to the young and trendy. We stop in a progressive-looking coffee shop, then another place that doubles as a used bookstore by day and a music venue by night. When those turn up nothing, we pop into a bar that sells only micro-brewed beer; a barbershop; and then an upscale burger restaurant. At each place, we show the photo of Titania and mention she's with the band ShakesPierre, but no one has seen her in the area. A few people have heard of the band, but even fewer have heard of Allan's murder, which isn't surprising since it had happened more than one hundred miles away and Pierre Von Strussen's fame as a one-hit wonder didn't give him the clout to break out beyond regional news.

A guy in the barbershop asks if Dede is in trouble with the law, and should the locals be concerned for their safety? I assure him that isn't the case. We are simply looking for her to make sure she's okay. That seems to placate him, but he still isn't able to help us.

Neither of us is hungry, but we decide to get a soda at the gourmet taco place attached to a microbrewery. It's casual and seems more approachable, more convivial than the upscale burger restaurant. There is a pool table in the center of the restaurant, and several televisions play different sports stations. Corrugated metal doors roll up to open onto a large patio. It gives the restaurant the feel of a party where people can hang out.

After we get our drinks, we infuse ourselves into the

crowd, showing Dede's photo and asking questions about the Clift cabin. But when all roads lead to dead ends, we decide to call Tess and ask her to drive out to the band house and discreetly ask Nick for more information.

In the meantime, we start at the top of the list I have compiled of the four cabins located within Johnson City. They are each within a ten-mile drive of the downtown area, but in different directions.

When we roll up the gravel drive of the first place, the Magnolia Cabins, we see a row of cabins lined up next to each other, three and three, with a seventh cabin in the middle that appears to serve as an office. The neon sign flashes NO VACANCY.

We try the office door, but it is locked. We knock, but no one answers.

A woman opens the door to the cabin to the left of the office.

"If you're looking to rent a place, we're full up. Don't get many vacancies here."

I glance around and see clothes hanging on a line. There is a barbeque grill in front of another cabin, and another flies a flag that says HOME SWEET HOME above a window box with an assortment of springy flowers, which are surely fake given the time of year. I get the impression that this is more of a long-term rental situation.

"Perchance, does a family by the name of Clift own this property?"

The woman shakes her head. "Nope. Chastain is their name. Bobby and Dottie Chastain. But they don't live on property."

I show her the photos of Dede and Byron that I showed the bartenders. The woman, who identifies herself as Maude, swears that she's never seen them in her life, and proceeds to name each of the other five occupants as she points to the respective cabins.

"Are they in trouble?" she asked.

"No, they're not," I say. "We just lost track of them and are trying to find them."

"Good. We don't want no trouble around here," she says.

As we are getting into the car, Tess calls. Jenna puts her on speaker.

"I took a break and drove out the house to talk to Nick," Tess says. "I'm standing on the front porch, and bad news, it appears that the band is gone. The house is locked up, and from what I can see, their bus isn't on the property."

"Did Jack say they could go?" I ask.

"I have no idea," Tess says. "I called you as soon as I realized the place was deserted."

"Did they leave any clues as to where they went?" Jenna asked.

"Not that I can see," Tess said. "But let me have a look around back."

"Be careful, Tess," I say.

"We have some news, too," says Jenna. "We toured Four Seasons's kitchen, and I am happy to report that the Briar Patch has nothing to worry about. I can't believe the arrogance of the Co Bros. thinking they can pass off store-bought bakes for French pastries. I have to wonder about their endgame. Is it to be the fastest closing business in Hemlock, because they appear to be on target?"

Tess laughed, and we also tell her about our conversation with the Hemlock Inn bartenders and how we learned that Byron and Titania left the bar together just after midnight Saturday morning.

"Now, we're trying to decide if they left Hemlock together," I say, "If so, did Titania, er Dede, go willingly? And did they have anything to do with Allan's murder?"

"Those are the burning questions," Tess says. "Whatever the case, I hope she's okay, and I hope they catch Allan's murderer fast. That reminds me. I have a huge favor to ask."

"Ask away," I say.

"Anything," says Jenna.

"I feel a little foolish, but I'm not quite ready to go back to my apartment yet. Do you mind if I crash at your place? I still have the spare key from yesterday and Bella is still there."

"Actually, you would be doing me a favor if you did," I say. "Would you mind taking the dogs out? It might be late when we get home."

The next cabin compound is as big a dead end as the

first. By this time, we're starving, so we decide to go back to the burger place and get some lunch and see what happens when we spend some time and money in the place.

It's after the lunch rush, and the hostess seats us at a booth in the bar area. There is only one other party in the restaurant, a table of six that looks as if it might be a business lunch wrapping up. Our server is a guy named Louis, who looks like he is around Jenna's age. It's clear from the moment we sit down that he thinks she is cute.

Louis's eyes light up. "Oh, hey. Well, my day just got exponentially better. How is yours going?"

His flirting is endearing, not at all creepy like Josh Collins, which probably has more to do with his cutthroat business attitude than his personal game.

Was that really just this morning? It seems light years ago.

After Louis puts in our orders for cheeseburgers and truffle fries, he hangs around our table, making easy conversation.

"Johnson City seems like a nice place," Jenna says.

"Yeah, I like it here," he says. "I'm from California, which is way different from Eastern Tennessee, but this is a nice change of pace."

"What brought you here?" Jenna asks.

"I'm in med school at East Tennessee State University."

They make small talk until he has to go pick up our order. When he comes back, Jenna pulls the trigger.

"This seems like a popular place," she says. "You must

get a lot of people in and out of here."

"Oh, yeah, from Wednesday night through the weekend, the place is packed," he says. "Sometimes there's an hour wait for a table."

"Have you ever seen this couple in here?" she asks.

Louis takes Jenna's phone and looks at the photos. "No, they don't look familiar. But let me ask around while you guys eat your burgers. Do you mind if I take your phone back to the kitchen?"

"Not at all."

He disappears through a set of doors next to the bar. A few minutes later, he returns with an older guy with silver hair and a moustache.

"I think we may have struck pay dirt," Louis says as he hands the phone back to Jenna. "This is Chet. He does food deliveries for the restaurant. He says this guy looks like the guy he delivered food to around noon today."

"What do you want with them?" Chet asks. But before she can answer, he adds, "On second thought, I don't care what your reason is. The little creep stiffed me after I drove all the way out to the Watauga River with his food. He paid the delivery fee because that's charged up front, but he didn't add a tip. When I told him I was using my own gas to bring his food, he told me to take it up with my boss and have him reimburse me out of the delivery fee. They're at a place called the River Cabins. Tell them Chet sent you."

He barks a laugh.

I use my phone to do a quick internet search while Chet and Louis are still standing here. Chet confirms that we have the right place.

We finish our burgers, and I leave both men hefty tips.

As we are walking out the door, Louis calls to Jenna, "I put my number in your phone. Call me the next time you're in town."

"He is cute," she says after we get back into the car. "If I didn't love Ian so much, I just might be spending more time in Johnson City."

It takes about fifteen minutes to get out to the River Cabins. They are a bit more remote than the other two places we've visited. They also seem to be uninhabited. The gate is shut, and a sign says CLOSED FOR THE WINTER.

"Maybe we should let Jack know we're here," Jenna says. "Would you please text him? This is not his jurisdiction, so he can't say you're interfering."

"I'm afraid he'll claim it's his jurisdiction or at least take it personally—especially if Byron or Dede turn out to be the perps and we followed them across the state line," I say. "He can be territorial that way."

"I really think he's just concerned that you'll get hurt or worse," Jenna says.

The knot in my stomach tightens. *Maybe we shouldn't have come here.* But... "I truly believe Dede didn't kill Allan," I say. "I have such a strong gut feeling that she can point us in the direction of who did. Why else would she have skipped out?"

"I'm with you. I don't believe she killed Allan, but we still need to be smart. I think letting Jack know would be the best thing to do."

I don't answer immediately, and Jenna says, "Do you want me to do it? I don't care if he yells at me, though one would think if he wanted you back in his life, he wouldn't yell at either of us."

"No, this is something I need to do," I say.

While Jenna gets out of the car to look at the gate, I take a deep breath and text Jack.

"Hi, Jack. Jenna and I followed a tip to find Titania, whose real name is Dede Clift. We're in Johnson City, TN at the River Cabins at 333 Old Pine Road. We may be back late… may I have a raincheck on dinner?"

I know he is going to be mad, so I turn off my phone and stick it in my pocket before he can text back. It will take him a couple of hours to get up here from Hemlock. But he's sure to come.

The gate must've been unlocked. Jenna is pushing it open, then she jumps back into the car and drives through.

The place is a neat compound with what looks like a large, new house and another structure that looks as if it is comprised of two older units tied together by a covered walkway that runs between the two. We park, get out of the car, and walk down the center walkway between the two cabins. I notice that the place is made to appear rustic, with nice touches such as framed maps of the state of Tennessee and a large tin star and other pieces of retro memorabilia nailed to the dark brown siding.

When we reach the back of the place, a nice, covered patio is next to a gravel area with a built-in grill and a permanent firepit. Beyond that, an embankment overlooks the babbling river that flows below. It would be a great place for a summertime family reunion.

But right now, the place looks deserted.

We start making our way toward the larger house off in the distance, separated by mature trees that line a cleared path.

"I don't know," I say. "I'm beginning to think this might have been a wild goose chase. Maybe they left or never even arrived. It looks like no one is here."

"If they're trying to disappear, that's probably the look they're going for."

We walk up the steps of the porch and knock on the door. No one answers.

I knock again, and Jenna peers into the window.

"There's a gap in the curtain," she says. "I saw movement. Someone is in there."

"Dede? Byron?" I call. "It's Maddie and Jenna. Please open the door. We just want to talk to you."

I listen, but all is quiet, until I hear the sound of footsteps and glance behind me.

Angel Ferguson has a gun to Jenna's head.

"Well, hello, ladies," Angel says. "This isn't your neighborhood. What are you doing up here?"

"Angel, let Jenna go." I put my hands up in the air. "Take me instead but let her go."

"I'm not letting anyone go," Angel says. "You shouldn't be here. But you are. We're going inside, and you are not going to cause any more trouble. Unless you want to end up like Allan. Allan got to be too much trouble, and I didn't have any choice but to do what I did."

"Why did you kill Allan?" I ask. "What did he do?"

"Stop talking," she hisses. "Get inside, or I swear I'll kill both of you."

Dear God, please help us. If you get us out of this alive, this will be my last case. My sleuthing days will be over for good.

As Angel walks Jenna over to the front door, I say a continuous prayer that her finger doesn't slip. My daughter is all I have left in this world. I can't lose her, too.

Because of that, I do exactly as Angel asks. I open the front door, which is unlocked, put my hands back in the air, and walk inside.

Angel motions us into the living room, which is off the foyer. I see Dede and Byron bound and gagged, tied to what looks like dining room chairs. They appeared to be unconscious.

"Oh, my gosh, are they alive?" I ask.

"Shut up and give me your cell phones," she says.

We comply.

"Do you have anything else on you that you'd like to give me?"

Yeah, a punch in the face.

"Like what?" I ask.

Angel narrows her eyes at me. "Stop playing dumb. It's not becoming."

"Clearly, we're not carrying purses. I don't know what else we'd have that would interest you. Feel free to search me."

I contemplate knocking the gun out of her hand if she tries to pat me down. She must realize that it isn't practical to keep the gun on Jenna and search my person, so instead, she says, "Turn around slowly so I can see your pockets."

I do as she asks.

"What is that bulge in your back right pocket?"

"It's the car keys." Jenna tossed them to me after we parked because she doesn't have pockets.

"Drop them on the floor and then kick them over to me."

Again, I comply. I'd hoped she would forget about the keys because they might have come in handy if she binds us to chairs like she has Dede and Byron.

"Now, sit down in that chair, Maddie." Angel motions with her head to one of two vacant chairs that seem to be placed there just for us. Was she dragging the chairs into the living room from the dining room when Jenna saw through motion the gap in the curtain?

I sit and Angel says, "Now, Jenna, you are going to tie your mother's hands behind her with that roll of duct tape over there on the coffee table. Make sure you bind her good and tight." Keeping the gun trained on Jenna, Angel pushes her forward. Jenna stumbles for a few steps but regains her balance.

Jenna binds my hands behind me. I am wracking my brain, trying to think of something I can do to make it possible to escape later. But Angel is watching us like a hawk. I don't want Jenna to do anything to set her off.

"Now, her legs," Angel says. "Tape each one to a chair leg."

When Jenna is finished, Angel instructs her to sit in the remaining chair and bind her own legs to the chair legs, then Angel sets down the gun and finishes Jenna's hands.

I am holding my breath, hoping my daughter doesn't try something heroic. Not now. While being tied up isn't ideal, we will figure this out later. I know we will. I have to keep believing.

Byron makes a sudden gasp—is he coming to—but his eyes remain closed. He was just drawing a breath. I shift my gaze to Dede and see the faintest hint of her chest moving up and down. Thank God, they are both alive.

"Angel, it doesn't have to be this way," I say. "You can let us all go and we will pretend like nothing ever happened."

She snort-laughs. "You and I both know that's not going to happen. Those two are down for the count right now.

And you should have followed Chief Bradley's instructions and butted out. If you had, you wouldn't be in this predicament, would you?"

"Will you at least tell me what's going on? Why did you kill Allan? And why are you holding Dede and Byron? What did they do to you? I thought you had a good thing going with the band."

"You are one nosy broad, aren't you, Maddie?"

"My mom is just as baffled as I am about why you would waste time doing this when you could be getting out of here," Jenna says.

Angel sneers. "Like mother, like daughter, I see."

She lowers the gun, which is a relief. "If I tell you, I'll have no choice but to have to kill you. Because you'll know too much."

"Why didn't you kill them?" Jenna jerks her head toward Dede and Byron.

Angel's eyes open wide. "Because they have something that belongs to me."

"What do they have?" I ask. "Maybe we can help you find it."

"You're not going to give me any peace until you know everything, are you, nosy? Unless I drug you like I drugged them. Now, there's a thought."

"What did you give them?" Jenna asks.

"Good, old-fashioned Rohypnol, or you probably know them as roofies," Angel says. "They took my stash and my money. So, I thought if they want my roofies so badly, then they should have some."

She barks a short laugh, then stops, looking irritated.

What in the world is Angel doing with a stash of roofies?

"So, if they took your drugs then you don't have any for us, do you?"

"Shut your mouth." She starts pacing, clearly agitated. "None of this would've happened if Allan hadn't gone back on his word.

"The shoe business was my idea," she says. "But it was just a cover. A front through which we were going to launder the money from the drugs. Then Allan got greedy. He wanted to reclaim his brand and start fresh. No way. Not when he was working for me."

"Was Allan selling drugs?" I ask.

"Ha! You bet he was. It was his side hustle, and he was about to get his skinny butt busted because he was sloppy. Sloppy and stupid. That's when I stepped in and showed him how to do it right. You see, it's great fun to be in a famous band that makes hit records, but the problem with that is, you have to keep making more hit records or your label dumps you. The hits just weren't happening and we were about to run out of money. So I helped Allan turn his itty-bitty side hustle into an enterprise.

"At first, we were funneling the funds through the band. But then a funny thing happened, the profits started getting so big that the band was no longer a safe cover. The feds wouldn't have to look very deep to realize these untalented losers weren't making that much cash. That's when I came up with the idea of Allan starting his own glam-rock shoe line.

"Little did I know that he would get greedy and want to make the sneaker venture legit."

She clucks her tongue. "I told him there was no way he was leaving me holding the bag while he went off to play shoe salesman. He just thought he was too good to get his hands any dirtier than they already were. So, I asked him, 'This is the thanks you're giving me after all I've done for you, keeping your butt out of jail?'"

Uh-uh. No way. He had to go. There was no way around it.

"Titania overheard me arguing with Allan before the gala. She thought she could use the info to blackmail me. It was bad enough that she wanted solo billing with the band—the chick can't sing to save her life—but I threw her that bone to shut her up. I figured we could use her until we found someone else to front the band.

"Then the little witch stole my money and my drugs and split. Thought she could disappear. The only reason I haven't offed her already is because she hid the drugs and money somewhere. I'm going to get back what belongs to me if it's the last thing I do. Then I'll deal with her."

Angel walks over and kicks Dede's leg.

"Where is my money?"

Dede stirs, but she doesn't wake up. Then a cell phone rings.

Angel reaches into her pocket and pulls out what looks like a burner phone.

"Where are you?" she barks.

I can hear the timbre of a male voice on the other end. Thanks to the inflection of his voice, I can make out a few words—*video, diner, police*—but I can't hear the entirety of what he says.

"Are you kidding me?" Angel screams.

The voice on the other end of the phone continues – *Questions. Police. Brother.*

"Listen to me, Josh, you had better not tell them anything, or I swear I will hunt you down and kill you, too."

Josh? Was she talking to Josh Collins?

Angel throws the phone at the wall and screams an obscenity.

"Was that Josh Collins?" I ask.

Angel turns her murderous eyes on me. Her face is crimson and vein on her forehead seems to pulse with every inhaled breath. I am bracing myself for her head to start spinning.

Or worse, that she is going to start shooting up the place. My mind races for a way to calm her down.

"Ugh, I should've warned you about that guy," I say. "He is such a loser. I didn't know you knew each other."

She blinks. The shift in conversation seems to have disarmed her—figuratively, at least.

Just when I think she's not going to take the bait and talk about Josh, she mutters, "You can't trust anyone. I should've known better. But no, he said he had it all figured out."

"What do you mean?" I ask.

"Josh Collins is my boyfriend and my dealer. He got his brother and sister-in-law to invest in this French bakery. He said it would be the perfect front for our… *venture*. Especially since Allan was being such a pain in the butt. With this, we wouldn't need him." She stamps her foot and lets loose a guttural growl. "But then Allan had to ruin it all. He said he was going to go to the cops if I didn't let him out and pay him off, and I said, 'How do I know you won't go to the cops anyway?'"

"Did Josh help you kill Allan?" Jenna asks.

"No, the wuss just wanted to throw money at the problem, but I told him, you don't know Allan like I do. Giving him money will be like feeding a stray cat. He will keep coming back and demanding more. No the cops are pressuring Josh to turn on me. They saw some surveillance from a diner after the gala."

That was Josh's alibi.

"Wait, you were there?"

Angel rolls her eyes. "I arrived later. God, I shouldn't have gone in the first place. But Josh said it would look good to his brother and sister-in-law since they'd only met me once before. I was supposed to come after I got the band back to the house."

"How did you get to the diner?" Jenna asks. "You didn't have a car."

She looks at my daughter like she's an idiot. "There was an old truck in the barn of that house that we rented. At first, I'd just planned on stopping by the house to change out of my dress and into something more comfortable before I met Josh at the diner, but the more I thought about it, I knew I needed to go find Allan and just get it over with. You see, I told Allan he needed to go see Tess and try to make things right. She might cause problems with the song."

Angel punctuates her words with a shrug. Her dark eyes look dead and unfocused.

A chill snakes up my spine at how casually she talked about murder.

"I knew this would be one of the few times I could get him alone." She continues. "I found the truck keys in a kitchen drawer.

"When I was on my way back to the hotel, I saw Allan stumbling down the sidewalk. I told him to get in the truck, but he wouldn't he said he was going to see Tess. So, I followed him."

"So, you planned to kill him on this trip," I say. That's why you rented the remote house?"

She purses her lips but doesn't answer.

"You purposely tried to frame Tess?" Jenna asks.

Angel laughs. "Not until I saw how badly Allan had pissed her off. When she said, right there in front of God and everyone, that she was going to make him sorry he ever came to Hemlock, well, that was a gift. That made it too easy. I knew he had stolen her song. So after Tess mouthed off about making him pay and then gave that woman the knife to cut off the security tags, I was just like, honey, thank you for being the gift that keeps giving."

"But so many people touched the knife," Jenna says. "How did it have only Tess's fingerprints on it?"

"Easy," Angel says with a wave of her hand. "Before I handed it back to Tess, I hid the knife in my purse, got a few slices of lemon from the bar, went into the bathroom, and polished that baby right up. I handled it with a napkin before I gave it back to her. Cleaning tip. The acid in lemons removes fingerprints."

"But how did you get the knife back?" I ask.

"Well, after I handed it to Tess, she set it down and ran off to do something else. I wrapped it in a napkin, put it in my purse and walked away with it. Here's another tip for you. If you act like you're supposed to be somewhere, people usually don't question what you're doing. Hey, I figured I might as well see if I could pull it off. If she would've taken the knife somewhere else, no biggie. Allan would've died of an unfortunate drug overdose out there in that farmhouse that's in the middle of nowhere. Look, enough chit-chat, I have to go out and move your car. If someone drives by and sees it, they might get suspicious. We wouldn't want that, would we?"

"But wait," I say. "So, Josh's brother and sister-in-law don't know anything about the murder or your extracurricular plans for the Four Seasons? They think it's a legit operation?"

"They know nothing. They're as naïve as a couple of babies. They were the money behind the operation. Josh and I were the worker bees."

"How were you going to work at the patisserie if you were on the road all the time with the band?" I ask.

"Oh, honey, the band's days are numbered. It's only a matter of time before I'll need to move on. Now, I'll be ready."

"So, did you have a hand in choosing the location for the Four Seasons?" Jenna asks. "I mean, it's right next to Tess's place. You tried to ruin her life with the band—did you have to try and take the bakery away from her, too?"

Angel's lips curve into an evil smile. "What can I say? Sometimes it's fun to take candy from a baby. Know what I mean?"

No, I don't.

But neither Jenna nor I answer.

Before Angel leaves the room, she cuts two pieces of duct tape and applies them to our mouths.

"When I open the front door," she says, "if I hear a peep out of either one of you, I will shoot Jenna when I come back inside."

She points the gun at Jenna's head but looks at me. "Bang," she says. "Don't test me, because I'm already wondering what I'm going to do with you once *Dede gives me back my money.*" She screams the last words. Then she shrugs. "Maybe I'll kill you all anyway. Getting rid of Allan wasn't that difficult. So, it wouldn't be that hard to do it again. You know what they say—in for a penny, in for a pound. If I get caught, the cops will put me away for him, what's four more? But I'll have to think about it while I'm outside."

She grabs the keys and our phones off the coffee table. "It might take me a minute. After I move the car, your phones need to go swimming in the river. Don't even think of trying anything funny." She lets herself out the front door.

It's hard to talk with tape over my mouth, but not impossible. "What are we going to do?" I ask.

The sound is muffled, but that's probably in our favor. There is no way Angel could hear us outside.

"I don't know," Jenna says. Then she starts using her weight to rock the chair. "I'm going to try to get closer to the window."

"It'll never work," Dede says. "And if she sees that you've moved the chair, it will just piss her off."

"How long have you been awake?" I ask.

"We were never asleep," Byron says. "She tried to roofie us so she could tie us up, but we both spit out the pills."

"We figured the longer we pretend to be knocked out, the more time the cops would have to get here. Nick knows we're here," Dede says. "When he texted to warn me that Angel had bolted right after you and Jenna left, he mentioned that the two of you were coming."

"How did Angel get here so fast?" I ask. "It seemed like the police still had a lot of questions when we were there."

Dede shrugs as well as she can with her hands bound behind her back. "They must've finished up pretty fast after you left. All I know is, Nick texted me and said he, Demetrius, and Angel were on the bus and headed toward Asheville, which is less than an hour away. She lives there and probably got her car and drove here. She hadn't been here very long before you two arrived."

"So if you saw Nick's texts, you have your phone?" Jenna asks.

"Well, I did until the Angel of death took it away. That's how she knew you two were on your way."

I nod. "Nick wasn't sure if you had your phone not. He said he tried to text you, but you didn't respond."

"Well, duh. Why would I take a chance on alerting Angel or the cops to where we were?"

"Thanks for letting us walk into a trap," I say.

"I don't have your numbers," Dede snipes. "I had no way of getting ahold of you."

"Maybe you could've called the police?" Jenna says.

"Should'ves, would'ves and could'ves are useless now.

Before Angel showed up with her gun, we were trying to figure out how to save our own skin."

"How did she find you?" I ask.

"The only thing I can think of is she must've seen the texts from Nick on my iPad," Dede says. "I should've grabbed it before we left, but there was no time."

"But you had time to grab Angel's money and drugs?" Jenna asks. "Where did you hide them?"

"I'm not telling you," Dede says. "It's my insurance policy that's going to get me out of here alive."

Now isn't the time to have an every-person-for-themselves attitude, but I am not going to try to school her in hostage situation etiquette. So we sit in silence for what seems an interminable amount of time, during which I have time to think. If, in fact, the texts from Nick came through on her iPad, there's a chance that Jack and his team have seen them. If so, there is a chance that he has alerted the local police and he or some of his officers might even have gotten on the road around the same time we did.

Finally, I hear footsteps on the porch, and voices.

"Who is that?" Dede asks. "Angel is pretty much a lone wolf."

"I can sort of see out the gap in the drapes," Jenna says. "I think it might be the cops."

That's all it takes for Dede to try with all her might to yell through the duct tape over her mouth. Her calls for *Help! Help! Help!* sound remarkably clear for someone with tape over her mouth. I chalk it up to the power of a singer's lungs. The rest of us start yelling as loudly as we can.

I see someone trying to look in through the scant gap in the drapes, and we all yell louder.

All of a sudden, Angel bounds inside the house and locks the door behind her.

"Shut up," she bellows.

The cop on the porch starts pounding on the door. "Police! Open the door, ma'am. All we want to do is talk to you. If you don't open the door, we will be forced to break it down."

I'm guessing that the police arrive when Angel was moving the car and she ran.

Angel grabs the gun and fires it into the floor. "I have four hostages in here. If you break down this door, at least one of them will die. So I'd think twice before you do anything stupid."

She starts pulling Jenna's chair toward the dining room window. I am trying to summon mother-strength, the fabled kind that helps moms lift cars off of toddlers or go without food and water for days because their babies need the nourishment. All I want is a burst of strength that will allow me to break through the tape binding my hands and legs. I press with all my might, to no avail. By this time, Angel has managed to scoot Jenna's chair directly in front of the window. She yanks open the curtain, ducking for cover so they won't shoot her.

"She will be the first one to go if you try anything funny," Angel screams.

Then, all is quiet on the front porch. My rational mind knows they are retreating to regroup and handle the hostage situation. But all my mother's adrenaline-laced panic knows that if she hurts my daughter, I will turn into the female version of the Incredible Hulk and bust through the tape. Fortified by that thought, I give one more mighty push—and the tape budges. It doesn't break, but it gives at my wrists and ankles. Now there's enough wiggle room that I might be able to slowly work my way loose.

Then what? I don't know. Dede and Byron are back to fake sleeping, which is probably the best thing for them to do. Dede has a way of riling up people, and she is probably the last one Angel would shoot, because Angel wants her money.

There is enough give in the tape that I can maneuver my wrist, which allows me to feel along the edge of the chair until I strike paydirt. The metal embellishment that connects the back of the chair to the seat has a rough spot. Even if it is only enough to weaken the edge of the tape, I hope that it affords me more room to eventually work my hands free.

I have no idea how much time passes since I've heard the cop talking through a bullhorn. It feels like hours. Angel has been quiet during the standoff, except to occasionally walk into the dining room from wherever she has been hiding in the house and sneak quick peeks out the window. Dede and

Byron are still feigning believable sleep from the dose of Rohypnol, and Angel obviously perceives me as no threat since she has the ultimate leverage over my behavior—my daughter. The time has allowed me to fray a good bit of my bondage.

Now, it seems the police force is back, and it sounds like they have brought the SWAT team.

"Angel Ferguson, come out with your hands up and we will not hurt you," calls a voice over a sound system.

Angel paces back and forth in the foyer between the living and dining rooms, muttering to herself. "I will kill them. I will. I swear I will do it if you make one wrong move."

Then someone from the outside drops a cellphone through the mail slot on the door.

It hasn't any more than landed when it starts ringing and the voice over the sound system demands, "Pick up the phone, Angel."

From my seat in the living room, I can see her holding the pistol in her right hand as she stares down at the ringing phone, considering whether or not to touch it. That's when a familiar face appears behind her and knocks the gun out of her hand, then kicks it away.

Jack.

I start bawling at the sight of him.

Jack, aided by the Johnson City Police Department, has come to our rescue.

ENDING ON A DIE NOTE

As the Johnson City Police take Angel away in handcuffs, I hug my daughter.

I try to inspect her wrists where the tape has bound them, but she pulls away.

"Mom, I'm fine." She smiles, but I can tell she's putting on a brave face as she follows one of the officers onto the front porch to give her statement. Byron and Dede are also talking to the police.

Jack and I are alone in the living room, and I don't realize I'm still crying until he reaches out and swipes away my tears with his thumb.

When I put my hand on his, he's shaking.

"You scared me to death." His voice is a raspy whisper that feels like home.

I look up at him, prepared to promise that I will never put myself or Jenna in such a dangerous position, that I'm swearing off real-life investigative work. Before I can utter a word, Jack bends down and his mouth covers mine.

The kiss is urgent and full of all the love I don't realize I've denied myself until this very moment.

I open my mouth and invite him in.

I know my feelings are fueled by emotion, but the life-or-death crisis has made my life flash before my eyes, and now, suddenly, everything snaps into sharp focus.

Why have I wasted so much time?

I know beyond a shadow of a doubt that I love this man. He just put his own life on the line to save my daughter and me. If that's not love…

But it's not just that, it's the way he has stood by me this entire time, giving me space when I've needed it, but being right there when I need him. It's been all about me these last two months. His kiss tells me the best way to repay him is for the two of us to start the rest of our lives together right now.

Epilogue

~ Maddie ~

January 1

I CLOSE MY laptop and smile at Jack as he walks toward our usual table in the corner of the Briar Patch cafe. It's a brand-new year. It's been three months since that fateful day in Johnson City, Tennessee, when Angel Ferguson took us hostage and held a gun to my daughter's head.

The old saying goes, you never feel more alive than after you tango with death.

If nothing else, that uncomfortable dance has helped me get my priorities straight. I guess that happens when you realize life is fragile and the things you hold dear can be taken from you in the blink of an eye.

You'd think I would've learned that lesson with Frank.

I know, right?

But it took seeing that deranged woman holding a gun to my Jenna's head and then watching the man I love—yes, I love Jack. More on that in a minute—but to see him rushing in there, risking his own life to save my sweet daughter… it has taken all that to make me wake up. Because I'll tell you, if anything had happened to her, well, they might as well have dug a grave right next to her for me, because I couldn't have gone on.

That's exactly the point. Life is short and fragile. Suddenly, I have realized it's ridiculous to waste another minute of my life sitting on the sideline waiting. Especially when I have no idea what I am waiting for.

Anyhow, they have arrested Angel for Allan's murder. And they have arrested Josh Collins as an accessory after the fact. Nick shared with the authorities that Dede had confided in him that she was afraid of Angel because of what she'd learned when she overheard the fight between Angel and Allan. With Dede's help and the information I gleaned during Angel's confession, they were able to locate her stash of drugs and add trafficking and money laundering to the menu of charges filed against both of them.

John Collins and his wife, Sally, maintain they knew nothing of Josh and Angel's plan to launder money through Four Seasons. Their intentions to try their hand at a French bakery were pure.

Josh bonded out of jail and his lawyer managed to work out a plea deal for him to inform on Angel, but Angel has been denied bail and is being held as she awaits trial.

It's clear that Allan Bossert got in way over his head. It is tragic and heartbreaking, because if Allan had done the right thing, he might still be alive today. Both he and Angel had seen the writing on the wall—the band ShakesPierre was at the end of their playlist. Shortly after Angel's arrest, the label dropped them since they hadn't scored another hit since "Tsunami," and, as with so many creative endeavors, you're only as good or relevant as your last project.

Speaking of "Tsunami," Ian has represented Tess and took her complaint to the record company. After some back and forth, they have agreed to not only compensate Tess as the songwriter, but they have given her full credit. She now has enough cash to get the Briar Patch Catering Company off the ground.

The band has decided to stay together with Dede and the boys. They call themselves Harem. Byron is their new manager. Although, it sounds as if Dede runs the show.

As you can see, a lot has happened over the past three months. I have some news myself.

I have decided to confine my sleuthing to the pages of my cozy mysteries. Especially since I'll be busy for the foreseeable future. About a month ago, a publisher acquired my Aubrey Christiansen mystery series. My hard work and perseverance in writing has paid off.

They've bought the entire five-book series. Now that the magical day I've always dreamed of has arrived, I will, indeed, be the most prolific overnight sensation ever to burst onto the cozy mystery scene.

Or so I like to joke.

Because one of the most important things I've learned is,

you can't take yourself too seriously. Life is too short. Once I figured that out, things shifted between Jack and me. They have been fantastic. And, yes, romantic. Really, it's as if the two months that we were apart never happened. I've moved on from living in the past, and thank goodness, Jack doesn't hold a grudge.

It was hard being apart, but that time was formative. He and I have talked about how we wouldn't be where we are today if not for where we've been.

I smile at that thought as Jack moves through the morning crowd at the Briar Patch.

When he reaches our table, he leans down and kisses me before taking a seat.

"Good morning, my love," I say. "How are you?"

"I'm doing splendidly, now that I'm here with you," he says.

One of the things I missed while we were apart is meeting right here every morning.

During that time, there was a Jack-sized hole in my heart. Remembering that feeling makes my breath hitch. Even though it's uncomfortable, anytime I'm tempted to take this man for granted, I will recall the days we spent apart.

"You okay?" he asks and laces his fingers through mine. He caresses the back of my hand with his thumb.

I smile. "I'm fine. Just in my head a little today."

He glances at his watch, then at the door. He drums his

fingers on the table.

While I might be a bit introspective this morning, he seems fidgety. Maybe he's impatient for his coffee.

I wave at Tess, who is delivering an order to a table close to us.

"Oh, hey, Jack," she says. "What can I get for y'all?"

"I'll have the usual," he says absentmindedly and glances at the door again.

The usual is coffee and whatever Tess has baked fresh that morning. Today, it's cinnamon donuts.

One thing I've learned from talking to Jack about police procedure research for my books is that often, you can find clues in how someone acts in the quiet moments. Sometimes, those actions speak louder than words.

I've got the feeling that something is up.

I am just about to ask him what's on his mind when Jenna and Ian walk into the bakery. It is unusual to see them together at this hour of the morning because they have separate places, and both have demanding jobs that usually require them in the office early. But one of the nice things about Ian moving to Hemlock and starting his own practice is that they can occasionally meet like this.

I wave at them, and they come over. "Good morning, you two. Please join us."

I won't blame them if they want their own table, but the Briar Patch is bustling today and they'll have to wait for a table to themselves.

"Thanks," Jenna says, and they claim the empty chairs.

They have just settled in when Valorie and Jack's sister, Angela, walk into the bakery. Angela is back for another visit. She and I have gotten great laughs out of how I thought she was *the other woman* when I saw her and Jack together at the gala. But she has become a good friend, and one of the biggest advocates of Jack and me.

"Look who's here," I say and motion them over, too. "How fun is this?"

Ian gets up and borrows chairs from the other tables that aren't using them. It is a tight squeeze, but everyone shifts, and we make room. By the time they are seated, Tess appears with five cups of coffee. I guess she saw the others arrive and is being proactive.

She distributes the cups and pours me a refill. Then lingers for a moment.

"Now that we're all here," Jack says. "I have something important to do."

He stands.

"Where are you going?" I ask.

It's not like him to duck out of a gathering of friends and family.

He reaches into his pocket and pulls out a tiny blue box. The next thing I know, he has dropped to one knee. A hush falls over the bakery.

Jack takes my hand, and I'm aware that every head in the place has turned to look at us.

"Madeleine Bell, I fell in love with you the first moment I set eyes on you, right here in this place. In fact, you were sitting at this very table."

My mind wants to make a snarky remark about my being so predictable, but my heart is overflowing, and I know if I open my mouth, the only thing that will come out will be an incoherent blubber. A happy blubber, of course, because I can't believe what is happening.

Until this very moment, I haven't realized how much I want a life—as husband and wife—with this man. And he is proposing right here in the place we met, in the place where we have gotten to know each other and fallen in love.

"Maddie, I promise to love you for the rest of my life," he says as he opens the small box in his hands. "Will you make me the happiest man on earth and be my wife?"

Well, of course, I throw my arms around him and say yes. I'm no fool. I tried to push this good man away. It wasn't really a test, but he has proven to me that he has staying power.

As he slides the ring onto my finger, our future flashes before my eyes. I know without a doubt that this man is home to stay.

The End

Want more? Check out Maddie and Jenna's latest adventure in *Maid of Dishonor*!

Join Tule Publishing's newsletter for more great reads and weekly deals!

Exclusive Excerpt: Maid of Dishonor

Book 4 in The Wedding Bell Mysteries

~ Maddie ~

THE SHRIEK REVERBERATES through the corridors of Gracewood Hall like a banshee portending death. I drop the ringbearer's pillow, which I'm sewing, and sprint toward the caterwauling.

"Why are you not wearing the nail polish I asked you to get, Betsy?" Bride-to-be and social media influencer London Brinks screams at her maid of honor.

Betsy stares at her glossy, deep green nails for a moment before she opens her mouth to answer, but London steamrolls over her.

"Did I or did I not explicitly tell you to buy Les Mains Hermes Nail Enamel in *Vert Egyptien*?"

London's southern accent murders the French words and Betsy smirks at her defiantly.

My daughter Jenna stands between them, arms bent at

the elbows, palms out, like a boxing referee keeping the fighters apart. She glances at me as I skid to a stop in the doorway.

"London," Jenna says. "Even if it's not Hermes, the nail polish Betsy is wearing will look lovely with her dress."

That is if one likes the color green.

London's face turns a cartoonish shade of deep red. I'm starting to worry that her head might explode when my mother, Gloria Phillips—everyone calls her Gigi—appears on the threshold next to me.

"What is all the racket about?" she asks.

I put a finger to my lips and nod toward the action, determined to let my daughter take care of her clients.

Gigi owns Gracewood Hall, the venue. I own Blissful Beginnings Bridal Salon. Jenna owns Champagne Events and Weddings. Despite my mothering instincts to step in and make everything right, I know I must stay in my lane. Jenna is more than capable of handling the situation.

"I said Hermes because I want Hermes." London's voice is guttural and low and shakes like a volcano ready to erupt. "What is so difficult to understand about that?"

Gigi, who could be Betty White's younger sister, returned to Hemlock, North Carolina, last year after her fourth husband passed away. It's good to have her home. I'm glad she turned to us in her grief instead of impulsively getting married again.

She's outlived all of her husbands and admits she's starting to feel like a black widow—even though they all died of natural causes, and she had nothing to do with their deaths. She doesn't want to get married again, but she still believes in love. So, she did the next best thing and purchased Gracewood Hall, the storied mansion located on a sprawling piece of property on the outskirts of Hemlock, North Carolina. She has turned it into a romantic wedding venue.

Hosting London Brinks's wedding as Gracewood Hall's inaugural event was Gigi's idea.

I would outfit the bride and groom.

Jenna would plan the wedding and reception.

Gigi would host the wedding—the first event at the newly renovated and reopened Gracewood Hall.

London Brinks would post about the event on her social media accounts, and her three million followers would clamor to book their weddings and events here, too.

Little did we know.

"I don't know what kind of skank-show weddings you coordinate, Jenna; my followers expect better than a low-rent imitation of my brand."

Despite my resolve, I start to step forward, but Gigi puts a hand on my arm, holding me back.

"We agreed my wedding would be classy, which means first-rate everything, right down to the Hermes nail polish. What is that tackiness on your fingers, Betsy? Don't tell me it's OPI."

"As a matter of fact, London, it is OPI." Betsy rolls her

eyes. "It's called *Stay off the Lawn!!* And that's with two exclamation points. You are totally off base."

"No, Betsy, you are," London yells. "You agreed to my standards when I let you be in the wedding. It was all good when you thought you'd get exposure at my expense—"

"How is anything at your expense?" Betsy yells back. "You get everything free. You get to wear the twenty-thousand-dollar bridal gown at no cost. You get the sixty-dollar Hermes nail polish free, but you expect me to go out and drop a fortune on a dress in a hideous shade of chartreuse that I will never in my life wear again. And then when I try to save a few bucks on nail polish, you treat me like a criminal."

She's right, the dress is chartreuse. While it's a fun, trendy color, it doesn't flatter many people. Certainly not Betsy, with her brassy blonde hair and pale skin. The color makes her look like she's nauseated.

"By the way," Betsy adds. "The Hermes nail polish doesn't even match the chartreuse dress."

"Get a manicurist in here right now," London barks at Jenna. "Have her redo Betsy's nails. I suppose she will have to use my bottle of Hermes since Betsy was too cheap to spring for a bottle of her own. If the manicurist charges, send the bill to her."

"Jenna, don't bother," Betsy says. "I quit. I've put up with her verbal abuse for months, and I'm done. I don't care if she is marrying my brother. I should've dropped out when the rest of the bridesmaids walked out on her, but I figured since I was the last woman standing, she'd get a clue and rein it in. No more. I've had enough."

"Oh, no," Jenna says. "Betsy, the wedding is in two days. Please don't go. London has pre-wedding jitters. She needs you more than ever right now." Jenna casts a pleading glance at the bride. "Right, London?"

"I don't need you, Betsy." London crosses her arms and turns her back on them. "Go on. Get out of here. Just *get*."

As London shoos her away with a swatting flick of her hand. Betsy picks up the garment bag that holds the bridesmaid dress. She shakes her head and mutters, "I am so out of here. I'm so over this."

While Jenna deals with London, I go after Betsy, hoping to convince her to change her mind and stick it out.

"Betsy, please don't go. It's your brother's wedding. Hang in there for two more days."

With one hand on the iron rail, Betsy stops at the top of the marble staircase leading down to the grand foyer and heaves a weary sigh. She looks exhausted, and I can feel the frustration emanating from her in waves.

We can hear London shrieking out here.

"Now, what am I supposed to do?" London wails. "Everyone is against me. Every single person who agreed to be in this wedding was doing it for the exposure they'd get on my social channels. They're all a bunch of users. I hate them. I hate them all."

"See what I mean?" Betsy says. "Would you want to stick around for two more days of that abuse? Oh, I'm sorry. I forgot you have no choice."

I weigh my words because I am firmly on Betsy's side. She's right. Jenna, Gigi, and I don't have a choice.

It's good that my daughter is handling London because I want to tell the spoiled brat that she should take a good, long look in the mirror. If she thinks the whole world is against her, the entire world might not be the problem.

Jenna is handling her, saying something in a low, soothing tone that I can't discern.

"London Brinks might be beautiful, but she is a monster. I truly think she would kill her mother if it would get her ahead."

"Honey, don't say that," Gigi says. "She just wants her big day to be perfect. Or at least the version of perfect she sees in her mind's eye."

"Good luck with that. Now, she won't have any bridesmaids. That's because no one can stand her. Sure, she's a social media influencer, but if people knew the real her… You saw how she acts. She has no regard for anyone. Green isn't my color. But she chose the dress and expected me to drop a grand on it like a pocket change. I will never wear that dress again, but she doesn't care. She thinks it looks rich and regal. I can't do it anymore, Maddie. I'm out."

I feel bad because I sold her the dress, but I thought everyone was on the same page. London would borrow a dress, and the bridal party would pay for their own. But Betsy is right. Even after I gave her a substantial discount, the maid of honor dress that London picked out still cost more than $1,000.

"How about if I refund your money and let you borrow the dress for the day?" I ask.

London picks that moment to come charging out of the room. "Give back the bracelet, you nasty little thief."

Betsy shrinks away, but London grabs her arm and yanks the golden rope bangle off her thin wrist. The force of London's manhandling causes Betsy to teeter on the top stair. I grab her arm to steady her. The last thing we need is someone to take a spill down the stairs.

"Be careful," I say. "If you two don't knock it off, someone will get hurt."

London ignores me and unleashes the enormity of her wrath on her sister-in-law-to-be.

"Don't you dare show up at any of the wedding festivities. If you do, security will throw you out. I don't care if Anson is your brother. Since you are abandoning me, you're not allowed to darken my big day with your ugly presence."

"Yeah, well, I can't believe my brother would marry someone like you. You're the ugly one. You'd probably sabotage your own wedding for the publicity."

London swats away Betsy's words, turns, and stomps back to the bride's room.

Betsy's brows raise, and she shakes her head. "You heard

her. If I show up, she will have security escort me out of my brother's wedding. I'd appreciate it if you would refund my money and let someone else beg, borrow, or steal the dress. I'm done."

She hands me the garment bag and walks down the stairs.

I turn and see Gigi standing there with her hands on her hips. She and I stare at each other.

"Well, seeing that neither of us is a size two, do you know where we can find a tiny stand-in who looks good in this strange shade of green?" Gigi asks.

I shrug, and we both head back to the bride's room, where Jenna is talking in low, serious tones to London. Miracle of miracles, bridezilla seems to be listening.

"Think about it, but don't take too long," Jenna says. "You're lucky she's free this weekend."

"What does she look like?" London asks petulantly.

Jenna holds up her phone and shows a picture of an attractive petite blonde.

London takes the phone and paces as she scrutinizes the image. "She's pretty and little. Maybe she's too pretty. My maid of honor can't be more attractive than I am. I might look like a moose standing next to her. You should know that, Jenna."

As Bridezilla scowls at the picture, I realize London isn't unattractive. She is big-boned and a little horsey-looking, which normally wouldn't even enter the equation because I don't judge women on their looks, but London is the one who brought up the potential replacement bridesmaid's looks.

Who is this person that Jenna's recommending? If London doesn't know what she looks like, Jenna must be suggesting someone to take Betsy's place as maid of honor.

Why should London be worried? She makes the most of her appearance, which is how she has become one of the world's top social media influencers. She's not too beautiful, but she's making the most of what she has. This, paired with her ease on camera, probably makes her seem relatable and approachable to her followers.

I wish I could pull her aside and tell her that while her online personality is friendly and helpful, her real-life disregard for others' feelings makes her unattractive.

"London, look," Jenna says in a steady, neutral voice. "Unless you know someone who can drop everything and come to Hemlock no later than tomorrow morning, you're out of options."

London bleats a *meh,* and with a flick of her wrist, she skims Jenna's phone back to her across the table. "I don't know."

My daughter barely catches it, saving the cell from sailing off the other end and smashing into the wall. I catch a barely perceptible flash of anger in my daughter's eyes.

She takes a deep breath before saying, "Of course, you don't have to have attendants. You could walk down the aisle solo and say it's the new trend, but it might look a little unbalanced since Anson still has ten groomsmen."

"You haven't told him that he needs to get rid of at least nine of them?" London bellows. "You were supposed to have already taken care of that. What in the world am I paying you for?"

"You aren't paying me, London," Jenna's voice is devoid of emotion, and I know my daughter well enough to realize it's taking every ounce of strength she possesses to keep from throttling this woman. "We negotiated an in-kind trade. Promo for services."

"Go tell him that he has to let everyone go," London insists.

Jenna closes her eyes and rubs her temples.

"Oh, dear," Gigi whispers.

"We need to figure out what to do first," Jenna says. "Do you realize it'll raise some eyebrows if you don't have at least one bridesmaid?"

"But you said I didn't have to have a bridesmaid."

"I'm saying one attendant makes a statement, but flying solo at your first wedding suggests something is wrong, especially since you have five flower girls and two ringbearers.

"You can get away with not having an attendant if you elope or if you have a small gathering, but when you invite five hundred people to a wedding, it's bound to raise some questions if the bride doesn't have any bridesmaids. People talk, and by people, I mean the ladies you've kicked out of the wedding."

Yes, five hundred people are invited to the wedding. Gracewood Hall can handle it, but we will burst at the seams.

"Everyone in the bridal party signed nondisclosures," London says. "They can't talk, or I will sue them."

Jenna levels her with a look that says, *yeah, right.*

The real story is bound to get out. Even if London embraced the theory there's no such thing as bad publicity, it wouldn't be a good look. It might damage London's brand.

That must be what the woman thinks because I sense her bravado wavering.

London flicks a piece of invisible lint off the sleeve of her blouse. "It seems so gauche to hire someone to pretend to be your friend."

I have to bite my tongue to avoid saying, "Well, honey, you've driven everyone else away. At this point, you're out of options."

But there is a note of vulnerability in her voice.

My diplomatic daughter says, "It's not gauche. It's a practical decision. You will be paying her to eliminate the drama. You want her to wear green Hermes nail polish? Consider it done. What do you say? Do you want to hire Kate for your big day?"

"What do you mean I'll be *paying* her?"

"Her services aren't free," Jenna says.

London makes a face as if this is the most ridiculous thing she's ever heard.

I'd heard about bridesmaids for hire, but I'd never known anyone who'd used the service. Clearly, Jenna had resources and had already started looking into the possibility.

"You'll have to pay her because she doesn't do work in exchange for promo," Jenna explains. "She has to be discreet. Think about it, if you promote Kate's business, you'll tell your audience you hired your maid of honor."

London blinks. Reality seems to be dawning.

"I can vouch for Kate. I went to college with her. She's a professional. Whatever backstory you all come up with—whether she's your lifelong childhood bestie or your sorority big sister, she will make everyone believe it's true. So, do you want to hire her to be your maid of honor?"

Find out what's next in *Maid of Dishonor!*

If you enjoyed *Ending on a Die Note*,
you'll love the next book in….

The Wedding Bell Mysteries series

Book 1: *Slay Bells Ring*

Book 2: *A Crime of Fashion*

Book 3: *Ending on a Die Note*

Book 4: *Maid of Dishonor*

Available now at your favorite online retailer!

Acknowledgments

Special thanks to Navy Chaplain Philip Anderson for explaining the heartbreaking process and protocol of family notification after the loss of a loved one in the line of duty. Love and gratitude to my daughter, Jennifer, for helping brainstorm the plot.

Love to my family for always being there.

More books by Nancy Robards Thompson

Whiskey River Christmas series

Book 3: *A Texas Christmas Homecoming*

Amalfi Night Billionaires series

Book 3: *The Billionaire's Bride*

Big Marietta Fair series

Book 1: *Beauty and the Cowboy*

Available now at your favorite online retailer!

About the Author

Award-winning author **Nancy Robards Thompson** has worked as a newspaper reporter, television show stand-in, production and casting assistant for movies, and in fashion and public relations. She started writing fiction seriously in 1997. Five years and four completed manuscripts later, she won the Romance Writers of America's Golden Heart award for unpublished writers and sold her first book the following year. Since then, Nancy has sold 30 books and found her calling doing what she loves most – writing romance and women's fiction full-time.

Thank you for reading

Ending on a Die Note

If you enjoyed this book, you can find more from all our great authors at TulePublishing.com, or from your favorite online retailer.

Made in United States
Troutdale, OR
08/18/2024